# ONE STEP FORWARD

## MARCIE FLINCHUM ATKINS

 VERSIFY
**Change the world, one word at a time.**
*An Imprint of HarperCollinsPublishers*

Versify® is an imprint of HarperCollins Publishers.

One Step Forward

Copyright © 2025 by Marcie Flinchum Atkins

All rights reserved. Manufactured in Harrisonburg, VA, United States
of America. No part of this book may be used or reproduced in any
manner whatsoever without written permission except in the case of brief
quotations embodied in critical articles and reviews. For information
address HarperCollins Children's Books, a division of HarperCollins
Publishers, 195 Broadway, New York, NY 10007.

www.epicreads.com

Library of Congress Control Number: 2023948487
ISBN 978-0-06-333931-6

Typography by Michelle Gengaro-Kokmen and Catherine Lee
24 25 26 27 28  LBC  5 4 3 2 1

First Edition

*For all the women who came before me—*
Thank you for enduring a long, difficult road
to give us the right to vote.

*For the reader—*
I hope you will always exercise your right to vote.

"The best protection a woman can have is courage."
—*Elizabeth Cady Stanton*

# I Slip on Deception
March 3, 1913

Our house of seven empties early.
Washington buzzes with extra people.
No one wants to be late—
> Father and Arthur leave for work.
> Rachel to Capitol Hill for her new job.
> Mother and Joy set up the Woman Suffrage Procession.

Sophie hides a little rolled-up paper in our special spot
in between the bricks
like she knows my plan—
> skip school
> watch the procession
> see what demanding suffrage requires.

I slip on Joy's navy-blue dress
roll up the too-long sleeves
put Sophie's paper in my coat pocket
add a hat
to appear older than my fourteen years—
able to blend in with a sea of suffragists.

Side streets descending to the Avenue fill
with more than workday hustle-bustle.
Frills of white skirts under coats
line up to march.
More women
than I can count—
the thrill of voting rights buzzes the air.

Spectators crowd.
Clouds of breath
mingle in the chill.

Too close.

I pull down my hat
tuck my chin into my scarf.

No one can know I'm here.

# SUFFRAGE FILLS THE STREETS

Washington, DC | March 1913

## Matilda Young

I might be the youngest of five—
days away from turning fifteen—
but I pay attention.

The fault line in our family—
men vs. women—
grows wider, especially because of
    SUFFRAGE.

## Someone in Our House Is Always Whispering

They whisper
about the women's march:
        *Woman Suffrage Procession.*

I'd like to see the thousands
of women
marching for their right to vote tomorrow.

*No, Matilda,*
*you cannot go.*
*You're too young.*
*It's too dangerous.*

Even my older brother, Arthur,
weighs in
with his no-place-for-a-young-girl nonsense.

Every exciting possibility
is always met with:
*too young*
*too dangerous.*

I slip a pamphlet from Mother's Bible—
        I invite myself.

## Someone in Our House Is Always Shouting

I try to finish my French assignment
but with four daughters
one son
and Mother and Father
crowded in the same space
I can't concentrate.

*Lucy Burns and Alice Paul*
*will help make a change,*
Joy, my oldest sister, says.
*Their Congressional Union*
*will get this suffrage amendment passed.*

*What's a Congressional Union?*
I whisper.
*If Father finds out I'm joining them*
*he'll come out from behind his newspaper*
*with a lecture.*

*It's a group of women*
*from the National American Woman Suffrage Association*
*pushing Congress*
*to pass an amendment*
*to give women the vote.*

Mother adds in,
*Miss Burns and Miss Paul learned their tactics*
*in England—*
*protesting in the streets,*
*breaking windows,*
*going to jail.*
*They.*
*Are.*
*Militant.*

*They*
*are*
*PASSIONATE,*
Joy shouts.
*Besides,*
*we need more than silver-haired women*
*fighting for the vote.*

Mother glares—
her head is somewhat silver.

The kitchen door creaks open.
*I got the job!*
Rachel says.
Joy and Mother keep arguing.

*I'm working for the senator,*
Rachel says a little louder.

I'm the only one who hears her.

*Better get used to the fighting,*
I tell her.
*Congressmen spend most of their time arguing.*

Maybe she'll know
how to get this amendment through Congress.

## Sophie Knows about Suffrage

I slip away from the shouting
stash the processional pamphlet
in our room
find Sophie, hiding—
always away

from whispering
and shouting.

*I don't want all my girls*
*to be suffragettes!*
Father's voice booms from downstairs.

*It's suffragists,*
Sophie says under her breath
correcting him without his knowledge.

*What?*
I say.

Sophie doesn't peek up from her book.
*A suffragist can be anyone—*
*man or woman—*
*who fights for suffrage.*

*Well, what's a suffragette?*
I ask.

Sophie puts down her book and sits up.
*Suffragette is an insult.*
*It diminishes someone.*
*It's what they called the British women*
*working for suffrage.*
*They accepted it,*
*but Americans want to be called*
*suffragists.*

*Father probably doesn't know*
*the difference.*

Just like me.

# Where Peter Stands

The next morning
on my way out
I run into Peter from next door.
Peter, who is always a step ahead of me
going to school.
Peter, who knows every person on our block—
and their business.

*Are you going to the procession?*

*No,*
I lie.

*Oh, but school's that way.*
He points toward Central High—
the opposite direction of where I'm headed.

*Are you going to school today?*
I ask.

*No, they've asked the Boy Scouts to help out.*
*Show the ladies where to go.*

I scowl at him.

He notices.
*I hear some women might be from out of town.*

I soften.

Is he a secret suffragist?
Will he help
or will he mock?

# To Be Carefree

I
stomp
frustrated
down
Seventh
toward
the
Avenue.
I
leave
Peter
in
my
wake
wondering
why
I
lied.
Why
can
he
go
to
the
march
but
I
have
to
sneak
conspire
deceive?
Boys
don't

have
to
be
protected
from
drunkards.
Boys
can
skip
school.
I
have
to
follow
rules.
What
better
place
for
a
young
woman
than
a
Woman
Suffrage
Procession?
I
belong
there.

## Pockets Are for Collections

I wait for the women to line up.
My coat pockets
are heavy with bits I collect—

feathers
rocks
buttons.
I find treasures every day
on my way to school
put them
into the top drawer
instead of clothes.

Sophie's rolled-up scraps
of wisdom
mingle among them.

The one I received after a fight with a friend:
*You must live through the storm to see a rainbow.*

After my first failed attempt at sewing:
*Masters become masters from failures.*

I rub the curled paper from this morning
between my fingers
then pull it out.

*Ignore the whisperers and the shouters. Find your own way.*

## The March Begins

A woman in flowing white robes
on a large white horse
leads the parade
holds her head high
guides this legion of women.
I hear her name in whispers along the sidewalk:
*Inez.*
*Inez Milholland.*

I try to keep my eyes on her
but people
            press
                    me
                            forward.

Police ignore the crowd
pressing in
on the parade line.

We are forced
to
walk
single
file
squeezedagainst
the sea of pushers.

A few men stop shoving to gawk
at Inez—
calm
in chaos.
Unbreakable.
Unshakable.
Strong.

Even as I stand
in this crowd
anonymous
I shake.
Where does she get the confidence?

## Make Room

A police whistle shrills.
The throng of men barely        part,
        making room for marchers.

Yellow silk banners ripple between
groups of women trying to stay together—
some hold signs
some wear white
fluttering underneath woolen coats.

Spectators sneer
curse.
I stand on tiptoe
behind the men
to see above them
        to
        inch
        my
        way
toward the women, but

        no.

Thereisnowaythroughthecrowd.

## Men for Women

Some men march with the women.
*Henpecko!*
a drunkard in the crowd shouts.
*Where are your skirts?*

Fists harden.
Chins jut.

Men marchers grit their teeth
bear the tongue-lashing.

One man in the crowd
spits tobacco
stains a suffragist's white blouse
laughs.

Another man
grabs an arm.
*Go home and make supper!*

She yanks herself

f          r          e          e.

The drunkards huddle together
clink their beers.
An older man stumbles out of the crowd
mumbles drunken nonsense
waves his hat around—

it's Mr. Franklin,
my father's Census Bureau boss.

I cover my face with my scarf.

Hide.

# I Bear Witness to Brave

One Negro woman walks
with the group from Illinois—

Mrs. Ida Wells-Barnett
I guess—
a suffragist
who told Miss Paul she wanted to march
with her state delegation.

Joy says Miss Paul wants everyone
included
but the suffrage fight
cannot be won without donations.
And the donors
want Negro women in the           back.

No one pulls Mrs. Wells-Barnett out.
She marches on.

As the procession goes on
I see Negro women
with white women in state delegations
from Delaware
New York
West Virginia
Michigan—

They don't hide.
They march to be seen.
They walk for more than suffrage.
They brave everything.

And I am
still
hiding.

## Unaddressed Evil

A voice spews
venom
at the Negro women
more horrific
than what other women
hear.

I turn to see Mr. Franklin
attacking
with words
that cut
pointing his finger
spittle showering.

I stand stunned
but the women march ahead
stoic
strong
unsurprised
at the vileness
of the crowd.

Like this has happened
before.

## A Swarm of Scoundrels

A scuffle starts with a shout
shoving
cursing.
Men move into the march
rip sashes
rip blouses

expose skin.

*Police!*
Someone shouts for help.

Police look up          do nothing.

*Police!*
There must be more police around.
Where are they?

I scan the crowd for Peter.
Where is his group of Scouts?

A man with a fistful of *Votes for Women* sashes
taunts
          yells
                    celebrates

with the crowd of the uncontrollable men.

The warning
about men on the Avenue
rings in my ears.

Then I see him.
Peter.
Pushing the crowd of men back
onto the sidewalk
where they belong.
He looks up at me
mouth agape.

## Hiding

I duck
behind a man in a tall top hat.

I pop up
for a peek.

Mr. Franklin is doing a drunken jig
alongside other men
including

Father

pointing and laughing
at the parade.

## Betrayal

The city spins.
I gasp for breath.
I blink again.

It's still Father.

## More Questions than Answers

I hustle home
before everyone returns.
Anger
bubbles then BOILS
until I'm
hot lava
r
  u
    s
     h
      i
       n
        g

          d
           o
            w
             n

the street.

Why would Father be there?
Do his mocking colleagues know his girls believe in suffrage?
Does he laugh at us outside our home?
Does he chide his own wife?

## Father's Deception

Father pretends like it's a normal evening—
paper reading
small talk with this family of mostly women.

*How was the procession?*
he asks Joy.

*Exhausting. Exhilarating. Excellent.*
She peels off her coat, scarf, hat, gloves
sinks into the chair.

I clench my fists
lock my jaw
teeth against teeth.
I want to lash out at him.

I want to tell everyone
what I saw—
our father
skipping work
drinking on the Avenue
making fun of suffragists.

I keep it to myself.

## What Does the Fight Look Like?

*What did you think of the procession?*
Joy whispers, even though the door
is closed.

*How did you know?*
I stammer.

Joy laughed.
*I saw you there
in the crowds.*

*How? There were thousands of people.*
Worry grew in my stomach.
If Joy saw me
who else did?

*Don't worry,*
Joy says.
*It was astonishing, wasn't it?*

*The women were brave,*
*unflappable.*

Joy nods and smiles.

*But who wants to be spat upon?*
*Have their clothes ripped?*
*Called names?*
*And whose side are the police on anyway?*
*They stood there*
*allowed the men to attack.*

Joy's smile fades.
*This isn't a gentle ask.*
*We must fight for the vote.*
*The result will be worth it.*

Joy is a dreamer.
A visionary.
An idealist.

*Why are men so afraid*
*of women getting the vote?*
I ask.

*They fear losing their power.*
*They don't realize*
*we already have power.*
*We just want to use it.*

*Is suffrage work*
*parades*

*fighting in the streets?*
*Being attacked?*

Joy laughs.
*No, most of it is not.*
*Most of it is writing letters*
*having conversations*
*sorting through information*
*building strategy.*

*So there are other*
*ways to be involved?*

*Yes,*
Joy says.

## The Day After
March 4, 1913

The new president
Woodrow Wilson
will be inaugurated
today.

A day without school
but I still go out.
Father
clutters my thoughts.
I walk it off.

I see Peter down the street
and am brave enough to ask,
*Did you rat me out?*
*To my father?*

He gives me an incredulous stare.
*Of course not.*
*Why would I do that?*

I let out a breath
I'd been holding since yesterday.
*Thank you!*

I head off in the other direction.
Peter calls out,
*Matilda, I brought you something.*
He hands me a Votes for Women button.
*I thought you might want it—*
*for one of your collections.*
*I'm with you ladies,*
*Matilda!*

My smile could reach the Potomac.


## What I Will Admit in the Dark
I finally tell my three sisters
in our room
in the dark.
*I saw Father on the Avenue*
*mocking suffragists*
*with other men.*

The sighs of my sisters
lift the weight of my secret.

*One day,*
Joy says,
*he'll change.*
*One day*
*when he gets out of the poisonous mindset*

*of his office*
*he'll realize*
*how wrong he is.*
*He'll be one of us.*

*One day,*
*we whisper.*

## Church and Chocolate

1.
We always
go to church—
the whole family—
without argument.
If we are hesitant about God
we keep it to ourselves.

2.
It's been nearly a week
since Father and I
deceived.
I'm not repentant.
From the lack of prayers on his lips
neither is he.

3.
We always
eat chocolate on Sundays—
Hershey's Kisses
purchased by Father.
*It's a sweet way to start the afternoon,*
Father always says
before reading and taking a Sunday afternoon nap.

# DARE TO DREAM

Washington, DC | April 1913–December 1916

## Half-Baked

Joy and I
pick up flyers from the printers
along with newsletters
and signs.
Arms loaded
we walk to Congressional Union headquarters.

The basement office
sits tucked under the street.
Footsteps of workers clomp above.
We focus
on the redhead.

Joy whispers to me,
*Lucy Burns.*
*She and Alice Paul are in charge.*

*Were they the ones who protested in England?*
I whisper back.

Joy nods.
*They met in a jail in London—*
*two Americans fighting for suffrage there.*

*Five thousand suffragists marched with us in the procession,*
Miss Burns says.
*Our Congressional Union will work toward an amendment,*
*establish our own newsletter,*
*welcome new, young suffragists.*

Miss Burns walks over to me
shakes my hand.

*Matilda Young,*
I stammer.

*Matilda, some of the women*
*call us half-baked,*
*saying we joined the cause*
*only after it became popular.*

*We are no such thing.*

## One Sentence

*What are suffragists really asking for?*
I ask Joy that night.

*One sentence,*
she says.
*One sentence added to the Constitution.*
She shows me:

> *The rights of citizens*
> *of the United States*
> *to vote*
> *shall not be denied*
> *or abridged*
> *by the United States*
> *or by any state*
> *on account of sex.*

This one sentence
could change
everything.

It seems so simple.

## Awake

I toss and twist in bed
suffrage on my mind.
Rachel whispers,
*Why can't you sleep?*

The room is still          silent.

*Joy and Miss Burns think*
*I should be a suffragist.*
*But I don't know yet.*

Another long          silence.

*It's okay not to know yet.*
*Sometimes you just have to take one step.*
*Then another.*

I think out loud
to the ceiling,
*Are there*
*part-time suffragists?*

More          silence.

Rachel says,
*You can be*
*any kind of suffragist*
*you want to be.*

Any kind of suffragist
leaves a lot of room
for possibilities.

# Chalking the Sidewalk
November 1913

A fall chill settles over the city—
I wish I'd remembered my scarf.

Men crowd the streets
after their government jobs finish for the day.

VOTES FOR WOMEN
chalked on the sidewalk
halts my hurry.

The white letters stand out—
even in a sea of feet.
Men scuttling by don't notice.

How can they not notice?

Until one does.

He scuffs it out
scrubs with the sole of his shoe.
I'm frozen
tongue-tied.

A police officer walks over to the scuffer.
*Don't even bother. We arrested the culprit already.*
*These ladies.*
He shakes his head.

*Wh-who did you arrest?*
I stammer.

*A Miss Burns.*
*She's their ringleader.*

I pick up a smidgen of leftover chalk
roll it around in my fingertips
for my collection
to remind me
even erasable words
can have extreme consequences.

## Give Me a Chance

*Did you hear about Miss Burns?*
I burst into the kitchen.

Joy cuts up onions, serves me
a you're-late glare.

*Miss Burns got arrested.*

No one is listening.
I help Mother with the carrots.

*For what?*
Joy says.

*Chalking the sidewalk.*

*It's just the beginning,*
Joy says.

*What do you mean?*

*There will be more*
                    *and more*
                                    *arrests.*

I want the chance
to do something meaningful
but I'm not sure I'm ready to go to jail
for suffrage.

Right now
all I can manage is

shaking.
Fury.
Silence.


## Mail Girl

Miss Burns welcomes me
at Congressional Union headquarters.

*You can open mail*
*in your spare time.*
*Even a girl in school*
*has time to go through mail.*

It definitely won't get me
arrested.

On Saturdays
I sort mail
listen to the women fill the room
with passionate arguments
decisions
voices not afraid to challenge.

I sit silently
trying to be useful.

# Losing Allies

*You may think we are all a set of old fogies*
*and perhaps we are,*
*but I, for one, thank heaven*
*that I am as much of an old fogy as I am,*
*for I think there are certain laws of order*
*which should be followed by everybody . . .*
*It requires a good deal more courage*
*to work steadily and steadfastly*
*for forty or fifty years to gain an end,*
*than it does to do an impulsive rash thing and lose it.*

—from Anna Howard Shaw,
a suffragist at NAWSA
where Mother is a member.

I feel the burn on my face
the slap on the wrist.

I put the letter in the pile for Miss Burns
to find later.

# Ode to Joy
February 1914

Mother is usually the calm one.
But not today—
she is fuming over cutting cabbage.

Father sits with the rest of us
in the living room.
I try to read
but it's too loud.

Father intervenes.
*Pipe down, will ya?*

*I will not pipe down,*
Mother retaliates.
*Not when our daughter*
*will land herself in jail.*
*And take Matilda with her.*

Mother's concerned about me
working in suffrage?
I don't want to go to a cockroach-infested jail
with criminals.
Surely Mother knows
I'm not that kind of girl.

*Jail?*
Father says.
*She's not in jail.*

*Not yet,*
Mother says.

*Things need to change,*
Joy bites back.
*We can't wait until men change their minds.*

I explain to Father,
*Mother's NAWSA friends and Joy's CU friends*
*are parting ways—*

*That's what you're mad about?*
Father asks.

*They're militant,*
Mother argues.

Mother thinks
opening mail
is militant?

*We are not militant,*
Joy shoots back.

> *Joy's conviction is so strong*
> *it destroys everything*
> *in its path,*
> Arthur says.

*Wait, do you admire her conviction*
*or despise it?*
Rachel asks.

> Arthur shocks us all.
> *She is indomitable.*

## Invading the Headlines

*Do you think we'll go to war in Europe?*
I ask Rachel
the open newspaper
splayed across the table.

With the Great War already underway
Wilson pledged to keep us out
but each day it seems
more likely
he'll break that promise.

She replies,
*I think it's inevitable.*

## Prayers
January 1915

Seven of us take up a pew.

While the minister speaks about sacrifice
I worry we will all know sacrifice
if we go to war.
War is everywhere but here.

Arthur stares ahead
eyes open
during the benediction.

Instead of reciting the prayer
I pray silently.
I ask God
to keep Arthur safe.

## Valentines
February 14, 1916

Joy and I are at Cameron House
in Lafayette Square headquarters
of the new National Woman's Party
across from the White House.

We work around a square table
making valentines.

To Representative Edward William Pou, from North Carolina
> *The rose is red*
> *the violet's blue*
> *but VOTES are better,*
> *Mr. Pou.*

To Representative William J. Cary, from Wisconsin

> *Cary, Cary, quite contrary*
> *How does your voting go?*
> *With pork barrel bills*
> *and other ills*
> *and your suffrage vote*
> *so slow.*

To Representative from Texas Robert Lee Henry and Rules
Committee Chair

> *H is for HURRY—*
>> *which Henry should do*
> *E is for EVERY—*
>> *which includes women too.*
> *N is for NOW—*
>> *the moment to act.*
> *R is for RULES—*
>> *which must bend to the fact.*
> *Y is for YOU—*
>> *with statesmanlike tact.*

To President Wilson

> *Will you be our Valentine*
> *if we will be your Valentines?*
>
> *Vote!*

Even in our serious, important work
in the midst of war
we embrace joy.

## Not Quite Ready for the World
June 1916

I wallow
for a week
after graduation
caught between the predictability of school
and the responsibility of work.
I have a diploma
declaring me ready
for the world
but I am unexpectedly
lost.

There's a note from Sophie
between the bricks:
*New beginnings are full of possibilities.*

Joy and Sophie
pull me out of bed
help me get dressed.

Everyone walks
around me
talks about me
right in front of me—

Enough,
I think.


## New Friends
I go to Cameron House
more often.

Every time I walk in
someone greets me by name.
*Matilda, you're here!*
I manage a smile
while I try to
remember their names.

So many dozens of women
coming in and out each week.
Some stay to work for months:

> Mabel Vernon from Delaware
> Julia Hurlbut from New Jersey
> Dora Lewis from Pennsylvania
> Mary Nolan from Florida
> Maud Younger from California

Do I call them by their first names?
Use Mrs. or Miss?
Mother insists on absolute politeness
but the NWP women
don't bother.
Mother's rules don't apply here.

They welcome me
as I tip between formality
and friendliness.

## Four More Years of Wilson
November 1916

He wins the presidency—
again.
The headlines
settle inside me.

Does Wilson in the White House
mean no to suffrage?

He told women:
*I wish you had the vote.*
He told the country:
*I kept us out of war.*

Four long years
since the march
four long years
lobbying congressmen.

Will his words
turn to actions?
Will his win
mean defeat
for the vote?

I waver between rage
and disbelief—
his wishes don't grant us suffrage.

## Picking Fights

We sit at the kitchen table
air thick with tension—

Arthur starts,
*How about that Wilson?*

All five of us women
bore holes into Arthur
with our eyes.

*We didn't choose him.*
Joy sneers.

> *I'll bet Mother supports Wilson,*
> *even if she can't vote,*
> Arthur jokes.

Mother shakes her head.
*This isn't funny, Arthur.*

> *Well, the men of the country chose well,*
> *didn't they?*
> Arthur turns to Father
> red in the face.
> Father didn't get to vote.
> Arthur didn't get to vote.

> *It's a sore spot, Son,*
> Father says.
> *I don't want to move out of Washington*
> *to vote.*

> Arthur opens his foolish mouth again.
> *You could move to Illinois.*
> *They allow women to vote.*

Sophie jumps out of her seat
leans across the table—

> *Enough!*
> Father bellows.

Sophie huffs back down.

> *If my gaggle of girls*
> *wants to fight for rights,*

*then let them do it.*
*I don't agree,*
*but I'm not going to try to stop them*
*anymore.*

Father
supports us?

Father pushes his chair back
retreats with his newspaper.

We sit in stunned
s    i    l    e    n    c    e
afraid to ask Father
what
who
changed his mind.
But I see Mother's sly smile.
I suspect
she's been feeding him a steady diet
of suffrage
or starvation.

Rachel chimes in,
*Arthur, are you*
*terrified*
*of women*
*getting power?*

Arthur leaves the table
his plate half-full.

This table might snap
under the weight
of our indignation.

# A Parting Gift
Mid-November 1916

Joy prepares to leave with Miss Paul—
Chicago-bound
for a suffrage speaking tour.

I catch Mother wiping away tears with a dishtowel
but we all know
we can't stop Joy.

Joy introduces me to her fellow suffragist friend Hazel Hunkins—
recently returned
        from dropping suffrage pamphlets
           out of planes.

*Hazel is unstoppable,*
Joy tells me.
*She will help you find your fire.*

But I'm just a girl
who opens the mail.

# Depth of Devotion

At Cameron House, Miss Burns paces.
*Inez,*
she says.
*deardeardearInez.*

Inez Milholland—
the invincible woman on the horse
with the flowing robes
at the procession.

Miss Burns tells us,
*Inez collapsed onstage*
*speaking at a suffrage event.*
*She did not get better.*

*Inez's last words were:*

>        *Mr. President,*
>        *how long must women wait*
>        *for liberty?*

*Wilson needs to hear those words.*

Some women's devotion to the cause
knows no limits—
even death.

# STANDING STILL

Washington, DC | December 1916–March 1917

## Honoring Inez

Suffragists gather in Lafayette Square—
three hundred women.
Tears flow as they prepare to honor Inez
to protest
before President Wilson.

I watch.

*Come with us.*
Mabel motions to me.

*But . . .*
I hesitate.
*I'm not really one of you.*
*I just*
*open the mail.*

Mabel comes close.
*That is important.*
*You*
*are*
*one*
*of*
*us.*

Her words
s
e
e
p
into me.

She grabs my hand.
I join the crowd
like I am one of them.

We swarm across the Avenue
descend upon the White House.

A few women go in
to speak
directly with the president
while
we
wait
outside.

Being in a crowd
lets me blend in—
I don't stand alone.

Silently following
doesn't make me a protestor.

The insiders stomp out
unsatisfied.
*He only wanted to comfort us,*
one woman shouts.

Miss Burns fumes,
*He didn't want to listen*
*to angry, dissatisfied suffragists*
*who use their*
*dead friend's words*
*to challenge him.*

## A New Tactic

Inside Cameron House, we fill
every available standing space.

We are close enough
to feel the next person's breath.

Everyone talks at once
whispers at first
then louder
and louder
until someone yells,
*Quiet!*

A hush falls.

*Let's bring the fight to the president,*
Harriet Stanton Blatch says.
*Every day.*
*We shall bring an army of sentinels,*
*suffragists bearing banners.*
*Let's stand at the White House gates*
*every day*
*until he changes his mind.*

Fight the president?
Protest in front of the White House?
Is any of this allowed?
What did I get myself into?

      Others oppose.
      *We aren't women of the streets.*

Opinions lob across the room
fighting to be heard.

*It's January.*
*You want us to stand outside in the cold all day?*

*We will take shifts.*

*Has anyone ever done this before?*

*No.*
*We will be the first.*

It is bold.
Brave.
Dangerous.


# Rose

I scoot toward the door
inching my way out.

Breathe.

Chilly air
clears my thoughts.

An older woman emerges
gasps in the cold air, and sighs.

*Are you all right?*
I ask.

She nods.
*I'm Rose Winslow.*

*Good to meet you, Miss Winslow.*
*I'm Matilda Young.*

*Please call me Rose.*

Rose.
She's old enough to be my mother.

*I was about your age*
*when I decided to join the cause.*

*Really?*

*Tuberculosis took me down*
*after working in a silk mill.*

*I've never been inside a factory,*
I admit.

*Long hours with no breaks.*
*Dangerous equipment.*
*Minimal pay.*

Rose's blunt list
makes suffrage work
seem luxurious.
*What brought you here?*
I ask.

*I knew I needed to fight to change factory conditions—*
*for the girls who are still there.*
*I am grateful for women who devote themselves*
*to suffrage full-time.*
*But what about the young girls*
*working six days a week*
*who don't have a dime or an hour to spare?*

*We have to fight*
*for those who cannot.*

Rose agrees.

Together
we brave the crowded room again.

## The Rules

The suffragists
decide they will picket the White House
all day
every day.

Suffragists will make history.

But there are rules.

>*Stand against the White House fence.*
>*Don't obstruct traffic.*
>*Don't get arrested.*
>*If the police tell you to move,*
>*go to the edge of the sidewalk.*
>*If they won't let you stand there,*
>*stand in the street.*
>*If they say you can't do that,*
>*walk up and down.*
>*Walk around the block.*
>*Keep on walking.*
>*Don't talk back.*
>*Keep silent.*
>
>*Don't come home*
>*until your time is up.*

## The Picket Question

Joy and I ride the trolley home.

*Are you going to picket?*
I finally ask her.

She looks around to see
who is watching
listening.

*Yes,*
she whispers,
*when I'm home.*
*I have trips coming up,*
*but when I'm here,*
*yes.*

*Are you ready to picket?*
Joy asks me.

*I don't know yet.*

## Picket Day 1

January 10, 1917

I am awake before dawn.

I'm eighteen, old enough
to make my way
in suffrage.
But still scared.

Joy scurries around the room.

Father knows what's happening today.
He mumbles his worries.

Mother soothes with coffee

        toast

           singing.


        Father talks loud enough for us
        to hear everywhere.
        *Joy, I need you to be careful.*
        *Don't take unnecessary risks.*

Rachel packs her sandwich for work.

Sophie and I listen from our room
get dressed
our worries echo Father's.


## Still My Feet

I'm a walker, not
      a stander.

Even though I'd like to join
      the pickets

I'm not sure they'd let me walk
      the sidewalks

pace with my
      banner.

I'd have to still my feet and my
      mind.

## The First Pickets

I watch from the balcony
as the line of pickets
leave Cameron House
with silk banners
purple
      gold
           white.

They lead with Inez's last words:

        MR. PRESIDENT,
        HOW LONG MUST WOMEN WAIT
        FOR LIBERTY?

People walk by
read
watch
whisper
wonder:
why are there women

in front of the White House?

## Wilson's Invitation

There's a hum of activity.
Ladies come in to get warm.
They switch off each hour—
four in
four out.

*President Wilson invited us in
to the White House
for hot chocolate,*
one of them says.

*What did you say?*
Miss Burns asks.

*Of course not.*
They laugh.

They are brave enough
to say

no

to the president of the United States.

I hurry into the kitchen
to make hot chocolate—
not as decadent
as the president's
but it doesn't leave a bitter taste
in one's mouth.


## I Choose to Wait

Joy survives the first day.

I wish she had insisted
I go with her
but she's leaving the choice
up to me.
I chose to watch the Silent Sentinels.

I sort mail
while other women
fight for our rights.

## What Happened
Nothing bad happened.
Nothing.
No police.
No arrests.
No ripped clothing.

I have no good reason
to sit out.

## The Press
I awake early the next morning
to read the paper before it gets used as kindling.
There's an article about the suffragists.

*Their purpose is to make it impossible*
*for the president to enter or leave the White House*
*without encountering a sentinel bearing some device*
*pleading the suffrage cause.*

We want to make it impossible for the public
to ignore our cause.
This is about more than the president.

## Private Letters
I accidentally open
Miss Paul's personal mail.
A letter from her mother:

*I wish to make a protest*
*against the methods*
*you are adopting*
*in annoying the President.*
*Surely the Cong. Union will not gain converts*

*by such undignified actions.*
*I hope thee will call it off.*

I slide the letter into the personal pile
hoping she doesn't notice
I've already read it.

Her mother sounds like
my mother.

## Come to Washington

I stay late at headquarters
skip dinner at home with my family.

Piles of letters
envelopes—
one hundred thousand of them
stacked up to my knees
in towers lean toward the walls.

Miss Paul and Miss Burns know we'll need help.

*Come to Washington,*
they encourage.
*Show your support for suffrage.*

They write a plea for members
across the country
to come to Washington
to let Wilson know
our stance.

I do my part by sealing
stamping
stacking.

# The Cause Moves Backward

After only a few weeks of protest
exhaustion hangs over
the women.

Shoulders slouch.
Eyes vacant.

Even Harriot Stanton Blatch
who dreamed up the Silent Sentinels
pushes away
resigns from her post
says we have gone too far.

Miss Burns—
the one who normally has enough fire
for everyone—
sits in the parlor
her hands over her eyes.

I offer her a cup of tea.

Her hands shake as she sips.

*Can I get you anything else?*
I ask.

*I'm okay,*
*just tired.*

*Why don't you go upstairs and rest?*
*I can stay.*

Miss Burns heads upstairs
her tea not even half finished.

## Suffrage Costs More than Money

A few days later
Miss Burns is gone—
home to Brooklyn
just as picketing picks up.

Burned out.
Sick.
Depressed.

If someone as passionate as Miss Burns
flames out
from the weight of fighting for suffrage
what will happen to the rest of us?

## Do They Know?

When
I
walk
home
from
Cameron
House
each
day
do
the
ones
who
pass
by
me
know?
Men

who
tip
their
hats?
Women
who
look
me
in
the
eyes?
Do
they
know
that
I'm
helping
suffragists?
Do
they
look
at
me
and
wonder
if
I'm
a
good
girl
or
a
rebel?
Do
the
women

hope
for
change?
I
think
about
each
person
I
see
and
wonder:
Are
you
for
us
or
against
us?

## Stories from the Line

I support the pickets—
help them with coats
hot chocolate
banners.

They switch places
come inside for a bit
layer on more clothing.

The stories they tell from the silence
are new every day.

A congressman asks,
*Why? Why are you here?*

One lady breaks her silence.
*The president asked us to concert public opinion*
*before we could expect anything of him;*
*we are concerting it.*

A woman scurries past and shouts,
*Keep it up!*

Hazel tells the best stories.
*Today a man came down with his son,*
*he said,*
*"I brought my little boy down*
*especially to see you girls.*
*I wanted him to see*
*history in the making!"*

I peel socks off frozen, blistered feet
add another log to the fire

and listen.

## The Kindness of Strangers

From the balcony at Cameron House
I see the White House gates
women with banners
watch spectators
see if trouble is stirring.

A line of ladies stands at attention
banners flapping in the breeze
suffering for suffrage.

A man
pushes a wheelbarrow

filled with bricks
wrapped in newspapers.
He lays them at their feet.

One by one
our ladies stand on toasted bricks
steam seeps up their skirts.

All the way from the balcony
I want to yell my thanks.

But I hold back.

## Sunday Pickets

Rose tells me
more about the factory girls

younger than me
working for minuscule paychecks

not enough to afford
rent and food

only Sundays off

no time or money to travel
to Washington to picket

the one thing that might improve
their chance at the ballot.

But they can't fight for it.

Rose requests a Sunday picket
a special day for factory girls

to voice their support.

Suffrage
shouldn't only be for the wealthy.

## Father's Line
February 18, 1917

I am ready early.

Father eats toast before church.
I button my coat.
*It's not time to leave yet,*
he says.

*I'm not going to church,*
I explain.
*There's a Sunday picket today
for working girls.*

*I don't care.
Today is rest and church.*
Crumbles of toast
come out of his angry lips.
Church is a line we do not cross.

*Father. These are girls.
Girls my age. Younger.
Who work for pennies in a factory.
Today is their only day.
Their only day to fight for the vote.*

*God will forgive me for missing church.*
*I cannot be forgiven for turning a blind eye*
*to the less fortunate.*

*Matilda!*

When I close the door
I know
it might not be open for me when I return.

## God's on My Side
I
holdmybreath
worried Father might come after me
yell down the street
alert the neighbors.

But
he
doesn't.

I
e     x     h     a     l     e.

Why does Father insist on his way
leave no room for thought?

I'm out of school—
old enough to skip church
for a cause
I think
our good Lord

would believe in.

# Picket Day 40
February 18, 1917

The girls wear their best Sunday dresses
and worry across their faces.

*What if my boss finds out?*
One voices the concern of many.

*My boss grumbled about the arrogance*
*of women who do this each day.*

*How would your boss know?*
I ask.
*You're from Philadelphia.*

*I've seen photographs in newspapers.*
*If someone takes our picture, we're sunk.*

I grasp her gloved hand
give it a squeeze.
*My father and my brother don't want me to be here either.*
*We all have people trying to stop us.*

She nods at me
opens her hand to take the banner.

*We must show them all*
*that no matter what they do,*
*we*
*will*
*fight.*

# Not All Mail Is Bad Mail

I tackle the mail pile again.
Ever since Mrs. Blatch resigned
I wait for repercussions—
fewer supporters
angry letters.
But instead
money falls from some envelopes—
a one
a five
a ten.

*For the cause*

*I wish I could picket with you*

*Please accept this with my apologies*

Miss Burns, back in Washington
sits at the table
looks at the piles I'm organizing.
*Every bit helps,*
she reminds me.

I read each letter
sort them—
       complaints
       support
       inquiries
       information.
Miss Burns looks at the neat piles.
*Do you want to do more?*

*I'm afraid*
*I'm not brave enough.*

*No one is brave enough.*
*We just take*
*one*
*step*
*at a time.*
*Forward.*

## Small Things I Do

I wait for the girls to return—
their already tired feet
aching from standing
on their only day off.

I add more logs
to the fire
stoke
a lingering flame
put on a pot of water
for hot tea.

I'm upstairs
tending to the scattered bedding
making room
for a few more girls tonight.
Some will be packed
wall to wall
in these spare rooms
even though most will head back tonight
for work tomorrow.

*Matilda keeps us all in shape,*
Rose tells the girls.

*I haven't gone to picket yet.*

*You might not be on the line,*
*but you are keeping spirits up.*
*That's no small thing.*

## Miracle

When I return home
after dark
the door is still open.

A single Hershey's Kiss
sits on the kitchen table.
I savor it.

## Another Miracle

The next morning
Father isn't waiting
for me.
No more lectures.
His newspaper
is splayed out on the table
open to an article—

> *In the past there have been no pickets*
> *before the White House on the Sabbath.*
> *Yesterday, however, the line was formed*
> *in order that working women,*
> *engaged with their occupations*
> *during the other days of the week,*
> *might have an opportunity to take part in the picketing.*
> *Carrying banners bearing the inscription,*
> *"Wage Earners,"*
> *a delegation of working women*
> *from the sweat shops and factories*

*of New York, Pennsylvania and Delaware*
*took their places in the picket line.*

—an acknowledgment
that yesterday had an impact.


## Tea with Hazel
February 24, 1917

Hazel and I sip tea
in between her time at the gates
talk about

fathers—
>mine just tolerates suffrage,
>hers doesn't think women can be doctors.
>Hazel got a degree in chemistry.
>*Our families may not be happy*
>*with our choices,*
>*but we do what fulfills us.*

Alice Paul—
>I am scared of her
>awed by her.
>Hazel calls her AP behind her back.

What's on the horizon—
>Hazel believes there will be
>fights
>arrests
>jail.

Things have been civil—
so far.
But Hazel might be right.

## Banner Minder

*I have a job for you,*
Miss Burns tells me
without asking if I want it.
*There's a warehouse that's painting banners*
*a few blocks away.*
*Pick up the banners each morning.*

I'll do anything
that gets me a little bit closer
to standing out there.
She nods at me—
a push to take
the next step.

## Spies

They stencil our messages
to Miss Burns's and Miss Paul's specifications.

When I arrive, one painter points her chin
toward two men in black coats
talking low
watching me.

*Spies,*
she whispers.
*That's what I think.*
*Spies who want to read the messages.*
Her raised eyebrows tell me everything.

I scoop up the banners
walk right past the men.
Who are they?
Police?
Men who work for the president?

They don't follow me.
But with every clack of my heels
I think I hear them behind me.


## Mrs. Terrell

Miss Paul invites Mrs. Mary Church Terrell
and her daughter, Phyllis,
both Negro women
from Washington,
to picket.

She tries to show the pickets
aren't just wealthy white women.

Mrs. Terrell hesitates.
Miss Paul assures her
we want her there.

But it's not
about Miss Paul
or the cold
or that she and her daughter
don't look like us.

The police
are always watching.
Mrs. Terrell doesn't want to risk her good standing
face punishment of jail.
Everyone knows if they end up in jail
it would be worse for them
than for us.

I hand Phyllis
a thermos of hot chocolate
and a gold-and-purple banner—

one without words.
Standing out there
is trouble enough.

## My Career

Miss Burns stops me one morning.
*Would you consider working here?*
*Full-time?*
*We'll pay you.*

*Yes.*
It's the step
forward
I need.

# ALL IN

Spring 1917–Fall 1917

# Wilson's Inauguration
March 4, 1917

Rain torments the city
but it doesn't stop
a thousand women
who've come for the formal swearing in—
they've been swearing at Wilson
for four years.

A rubber company
outfits everyone
for the incessant rain—
hats, raincoats, boots.

Seventy-year-old
Dora Lewis
puts her arm through mine
pulling me along.
*You're going with me.*
*Your young legs will help me steady myself.*
*It's slick out here.*

I've never seen Mrs. Lewis hesitate
with her steps—
even in the rain.
But her resolve will help steady
my racing heart.


# A Little Rain
Vida Milholland,
Inez's sister,
leads with her late sister's words:

MR. PRESIDENT,
HOW LONG MUST WOMEN
WAIT FOR LIBERTY?

Another banner says:

WE DEMAND AN AMENDMENT
TO THE CONSTITUTION
OF THE UNITED STATES
ENFRANCHISING WOMEN.

Police watch
wait for trouble.
We proceed to the main gates of the White House.

Locked.

The second gate.

Locked.

The last gate.

Locked.

We convince a guard
to petition the president's secretary.
He comes back
sheepish, in trouble
for leaving his post.

We march
around the White House
four times
for two hours.

We are soaked
from banners
to stockings

hands sticky
with varnish
from the wet wooden banner poles.
Our skirts hang
heavy.

When we see
the presidential limousine
the Wilsons
won't even look at us
on their way to the Capitol.

The sting of rain mixes
with the sting of injustice.

Some of these women
fought for suffrage
before I was born.

A little rain
doesn't dampen
their spirits
or wash away their beliefs.

A little rain
is a reminder
that I don't have to wait
for perfect conditions
to be brave.

# We Stop
March 6, 1917

Wilson begins his second term.
Congress is not in session yet
no official business—
including suffrage—
is being considered
or voted on.

There is silence at the White House gates—
        no pickets
        no banners
        no grumblers who oppose.
Our ladies take a break from the daily slog
of standing
silent.

I pour myself into my work—
        mail
        organizing banners
        helping with the *Suffragist*,
        our weekly newsletter.
I take the occasional evening off
usually too tired for fun.


# Picket Day 84
April 3, 1917

I choose a gold-and-purple banner—
no words
just solidarity
with my sisters.

I pin the Votes for Women button
from Peter
to my blouse.

One day,
I'll shout my words
from a banner.

## I Stand

### 1.

I imagined standing at the gates
banner in hand—tall and proud.
I imagined I'd be strong
in spite of cursing crowds
spewing their hate at me.

### 2.

Here I stand.
Pride and stubbornness
swell within me
making me unmovable.
I ignore the stares
glares trying to cut me.
I stand firm.

### 3.

After a bit, my toes ache
inside my stiff black shoes
My shoulders tighten
from holding the banner so still.

### 4.

I stand
for all the girls who can't.

## The Slowness of Change

Four years ago
women marched
for the vote.

They pressed
the new president
for support.

Four years later
I'm eighteen
and should feel less scared
more assured.

Four years later
the president is still rigid.

I share something in common with the president—
slow to become brave
slow to take a stand.

Maybe there's hope for both of us.


## Did They Notice?

There were no celebrations—
no encouragements
no nods of acknowledgment
when I put my banner away for the day.
I'm not even sure anyone noticed.

Joy is still out traveling for suffrage
so there's not even a sisterly nod.
I don't need praise from these veteran suffrage fighters.

(But a smile would be nice.)

# Rachel's Attention to War

Rachel spends her evenings
spread over the news
reading every article.
Every headline
hints at our path to war.

*Don't you need a break?*
I ask.

*A break from what?*

*Talk of war.*

*Our men are going to be called up to fight, Matilda.*
*We can take no breaks.*

Rachel's boss,
Senator La Follette,
a suffragist himself
must appreciate her sharp mind
as his secretary.

I'm grateful the Rachels of the world
work on Capitol Hill.

I just hope they remember
suffrage
while the world is at war.

# War on Suffrage

April 5, 1917

War with Europe looms
on the horizon.

*What will happen
to suffrage if we go to war?*
I dare to ask a roomful of weary picketers.

Miss Burns tells me,
*Through the Civil War,
suffrage waited.
Our sisters
gave themselves to the war effort.*

Mrs. Lewis says,
*Women withdrew from the fight
because it was the Negro's Hour.
Our time was yet to come.*

Miss Paul says,
*We will not pause
for war.
We will not wait for men to stop fighting
to wage our war.*

Mrs. Lewis raises her voice.
*We wait no more.
We don't want our granddaughters
to have to wait.*

Their determination
their righteous anger
their piercing eyes
contain a fire

a fight
that will push suffrage at any cost.

What will it mean for the girls on the line?
Breaking silence?
Fighting back?
Arrests?

## The Great War

April 6, 1917

The Great War
waged in Europe
until today.

Rachel barely sleeps.
Some evenings
we share a spread-out newspaper.

President Wilson explains,
America, too, must go to war.

*We shall fight for the things*
*which we have always carried*
*nearest our hearts—*
*for democracy,*
*for the right of those who submit to authority*
*to have a voice in their own Governments.*

How can we be fighting
for democracy in Europe
when women here
don't have a voice?

## One Late Night

I thought everyone was asleep
but me.

Sophie pipes up
from under the covers.
*I'm going to train as a nurse,*
*so I can join the war effort.*

She's been so quiet lately
contemplative.

*Soph—*
Rachel tries to step in.

*You can't talk me out of it.*

*I know,*
Rachel says.
*I worry.*

Joy travels the country for suffrage—
living out her dreams
while we lie here
wishing for our futures.

*I want to go to Europe*
*where our troops will need nurses,*
Sophie says.

I confess to my sisters,
*I want to keep standing in front of the White House*
*as a Silent Sentinel—*

*Matilda!*
Sophie squeals quietly.

*You did it!*
Rachel whispers.

*I want to keep doing it,*
*not lose my nerve.*

We lie there for a few moments.
Our dreams swirl in the silence.
*I also want to save my money—*
*have my own place.*

Sophie says,
*Big dreams.*

No one can stop us.


## Rally the Troops

The Selective Service tells men
to register
to wait for their number
to fight.

War posters tell women:
>           knit socks and scarves for soldiers
>           conserve food
>           serve in jobs while men are away.

The pressure—
the message—
is clear:
Don't be selfish.
Serve your country.

# War Work

Mother signs up to help the Red Cross
feeding soldiers
assembling comfort kits to be shipped overseas.

Sophie's gone from home
training
waiting for her turn to serve.

Rachel comes home from the Hill
collapses.
She can barely keep
                her
                     eyes
                        open.

I serve my country
and fight for suffrage.

*How are things at headquarters?*
Mother asks.

*I stood on the picket line for the first time.*

Mother's knitting hands stop.
I prepare for a scolding.

*The actions you take each day*
*add up*
*even if they seem small.*

A smidgen of guilt creeps in
as she knits.
I could help her
but I save my energy
for suffrage.

## Day after Day

Four months
since the ladies
took a stand at the White House gates.
The weather has warmed a bit
but the monotony of the daily pickets
has not changed.

Grab a banner.
March.
Stand.
Stay silent.
Watch as the hours roll by.
Come back.
Switch off.
Stand again.

I wish I could
bring a book
because
standing
is boring.

There is nothing special
about the day-to-day pickets
anymore.

Miss Paul warns us not to grow weary—
gentle pressure each day
gets us closer to our goal.

But does it?

My tight grip on the banner poles
callouses my hands.
Each time I put salve on them

I wonder
if the president
even notices the army of women
at his gates
or if now we are simply
gawdy decorations.

## Domestic Turmoil

War is here
in our house.

Sophie is assigned
to the Army Nurse Corps.
She ships off
soon.

The always-busy house of seven
will be a somber six
might be a slim five
if Arthur gets called up.

Mother's tearful eyes
Father's distraught face
turns my stomach into knots.

We eat our dinner together
but a cloud of silence hovers—
even a joke
might turn to sobs.

## Wounds

When the silence breaks
and whispers of war begin
Joy leaves the table.

*She doesn't believe in war,*
*any war,*
Sophie says.

> *How can anyone not support*
> *our country, our president*
> *at a time of war?*
> Father says.
> *Must be that Merrill Rogers fellow,*
> *working for that antiwar magazine.*
> *He's made her antiwar.*

*No man changed her,*
Rachel explains.
*This is who Joy is.*

*We're fighting for rights*
*in Europe*
*before we have our own here,*
*and she had those opinions long before*
*she met Merrill,*
I insist.

> *Well, none of us have voting rights here.*
> Arthur says.
> *You ladies can get married,*
> *move out West*
> *where you can vote.*

Our eyes burn into him.
*Still trying to get rid of us?*
Rachel says.

Sophie chimes in,
*Don't worry,*
*soon you'll have one less sister to deal with.*

Father's face is a rising thermometer.
*I provide for you—*
*food,*
*a place to sleep,*
*but all you do is argue.*
*Arthur,*
*stop picking fights with*
*your sisters.*

Father leaves the table
handkerchief out of his pocket
disappears into the living room
hides behind his paper.

Sophie and I still sit
around a table of empty dishes.
She grabs my hand.
*The war will not tear us apart,*
she promises.

Never.


## Deepest Cuts

I walk into Cameron House
and into a fight.

Rose whispers to me,
*Mrs. Carrie Chapman Catt, from NAWSA,*
she points at the lady confronting Miss Paul.

I've heard of her.

*We will not lay down our banners,*
Miss Paul says through gritted teeth.

*Giving up suffrage during the Civil War*
*was a mistake.*

Mrs. Catt lashes out
and I only overhear pieces of it:
*unwise*
*unpatriotic*
*unprofitable to the cause.*

But being nice
patient
tolerant
hasn't given us the vote.

Alice Paul
Carrie Chapman Catt
Harriet Stanton Blatch
all want the vote
but their friendship is in unmendable tatters.

We can shake off
strangers' words.

We can burn
disapproving letters
from other women
in our fireplace
to keep Cameron House warm.

But the cuts of disapproval
from friends
fester.

# Bedtime Reading
April 19, 1917

Rachel and I read at the table—
she with the *Post*
me with the *Suffragist*.

She starts
snickering.

*Bad Manners, Mad Banners*

*Editor Post: One thing that strikes the visitor to Washington as
somewhat out of place is the undue liberty allowed those suffragettes
who foolishly stand at the gates of the President's house—the silent
sentinels, I believe they are called.*

*It seems to me that the President, especially in these trying days,
should be spared every annoyance that can possibly be averted, and
surely the cause of woman suffrage is not helped by resorting to these
bad manners and mad banners.*

*George Foster, New York*

We stifle our giggles
so we don't wake Father.

I clip this one for my collection.
Years from now, we'll still be laughing about it.


# To Be Like Hazel
Hazel
is here
all day
every day.

She carries the picket banners
each time
ignoring the jeers.

She's even made friends
with people who pass by
every day—
> the sailor who winks at her
> the limousine ladies who wave their handkerchiefs at her
> the impish boy who sneers at her.

She gives them her Vassar sass
waves and smiles
and puts a good face on suffrage.

She's not afraid to speak up
not afraid to hold words on her banner.

Each time I go out to picket
I shake—
worried that someone will ask me a question
or police will whir through in their Black Marias.
I imagine the worst.
My thoughts consume me.

If only I could be more
like Hazel.

## Life without Sophie
May 1, 1917

Sophie comes home
from training
to say goodbye.
The dread in my stomach
burns more than ever

now that she'll be leaving
the country.

*France,*
I hear Mother whisper.
*They're shipping her to France.*

> *May God protect her,*
> Father prays aloud.
> *Keep her safe in this war.*

I have never known my room
without Sophie—
it's empty without her.

She hugs each of us.
I am the last.
*Keep fighting for what you want,*
she whispers,
and hands me a Red Cross button.
*For your collection.*

I nod through tears.
She waves goodbye.
The rest of the family
scatters before the tears fall.

## What She Left Behind

I go straight to our room
after the goodbyes
dry my tears in private
wallow in the selfishness
of wanting her to stay
knowing she's exactly where
she wants to be.

Above my pillow
in the gap between the bricks
are several rolled-up notes.

I can't bear to open
even one.
They need to last
until she returns.

## Two Kinds of Men

I walk out onto Lafayette Square
with a contentious banner:
DEMOCRACY
SHOULD BEGIN AT HOME.

Warmer spring weather
brings larger crowds
to watch us picket.

*The democracy of the world
is at stake!
How dare you
embarrass the president!*

Embarrass the president?
The signs haven't moved him yet.
That's why we're still here.

*You are impossible!
You unpatriotic
gang of women!*

The banners with words
provoke.

The yelling
the venom
aimed at me
is hard to take silently.

In the mob of men—

Arthur.

Sees me.
Sees me with
my banner.
His face
reddens
as he hides
behind the mob
moves on.

Behind the angry swarm
is one man—
older
grayer
kinder.

He says,
*Girls, you are right.*
*You all got to have some rights.*

A stranger
can be kinder
than kin.

## My Voice

My hands tremble
from the shouting
from seeing my own brother
embrace the hostility.

I race to my room—
home before Arthur.
What will I say to him?

I slip a paper
out of the brick
hoping Sophie prophesied
this moment.

*Your voice can start as a whisper.*

The door opens downstairs.


## Defying Expectations

*Arthur,*
my voice barely scratches above a whisper.
Surprise
in his eyes.

He says nothing.

*Arthur,*
my voice
cracks.
*Let's go for a walk.*

> *Well, I told Mother I'd help.*
> He points to the basket of vegetables
> on the table—

*Go,*
Mother waves him off.
*Go.*

## Walking with Arthur

I kill him with
silence.

> *Where are we going?*
> he asks.

*For a walk.*
He clearly doesn't understand the point
of a walk.
I say
nothing
for three blocks.

> He finally talks.
> *I didn't realize people were so angry,*
> *and I didn't want to be a part*
> *but I got stuck in the mob*
> *and couldn't escape.*
> *I don't agree with what you're doing*
> *but I'd never hurt you or your friends.*
> *And why are you*
> *carrying banners?*
> *I thought you*
> *just opened and sorted mail.*
> *You're a picket now!*

His words come out fast.
Excuses ooze.

I let him finish before I speak—
fire
coursing through my veins.

*I want a voice.*
*Even if you'd rather*
*I didn't use it.*
*I am not going to STOP.*

We
walk
in
silence
all
the
way
home.

# The Only Time Arthur Has Ever Been Right

I can tell Arthur has been thinking
when he stands at the door to my room.
He pauses
before he speaks.

*I think being silent*
*won't work.*

Warmth rises in my cheeks.
I take deep breaths
slow the anger inside.

*You may have to speak up,*
he says.

He's right
even if I don't want to admit it.

# Picket Day 162
June 20, 1917

When I pick up today's banners from the painters
I know
they will agitate.
I worry
we are going too far.

Russian diplomats will meet with President Wilson
and see our
targeted message.

When I unfurl the banners
the women don't hesitate
but we all know
these barbs
will bring backlash.

> TO THE RUSSIAN MISSION:
> PRESIDENT WILSON AND ENVOY ROOT
> ARE DECEIVING RUSSIA.

Mrs. Lewis and Miss Burns want to show
America's hypocrisy.

> THEY SAY, "WE ARE A DEMOCRACY.
> HELP US WIN A WAR
> SO THAT DEMOCRACY MAY SURVIVE."
> WE, THE WOMEN OF AMERICA,
> TELL YOU THAT AMERICA IS NOT
> A DEMOCRACY.

Russian diplomats drive
through the White House gates
without pausing to read.

TWENTY MILLION AMERICAN WOMEN
ARE DENIED THE RIGHT TO VOTE.
PRESIDENT WILSON IS THE CHIEF OPPONENT
OF THE NATIONAL ENFRANCHISEMENT.

But to the hundreds of government workers
on lunch break, the banners are not a blur.

HELP US MAKE THIS NATION REALLY FREE.
TELL OUR GOVERNMENT THAT IT MUST
LIBERATE ITS PEOPLE BEFORE IT CAN CLAIM
FREE RUSSIA AS AN ALLY.

The crowd screams,
*Traitors!*
*Treason!*

## Clash
June 20, 1917

I watch out the window
wait for my shift
to take the banner.
The men slash
a Russian banner.
Pieces lay on the sidewalk
while Miss Burns and Mrs. Lewis
stand
solemn.

Men in the crowd spit on Hazel—
her banner in tatters.

Our women cling to barren banner posts
police shuffle around

picking up pieces
as evidence.

Our pickets hobble back to Cameron House
I meet them on the street
wrap shawls around torn clothing
remind Mrs. Lewis to breathe.

*Despicable women!*
we hear the shouts.
*We're at war, you know.*
Miss Burns stares at them—
hard—
even as the redness creeps into her cheeks.

I see a scrap of banner
left by the police.
I tuck it into my waistband
save it for my collection.

## We Are Mocked

The words
pound in my ears
> *impossible*
> *unpatriotic*
> *traitors*
> *despicable*
each is a lash
on our resolve.

Sophie's words hide in the hole.
I try to ration them,
only unfurling them on my most desperate days.

*Mockers have no moral compass.*

The hate-filled words
still rattle around in my head
until I refuse them space.
They can take up residence elsewhere.

## Reporting the Facts
June 21, 1917

1.
The *Washington Post*
should give news of the city
without bias.

2.
They don't just give facts—
they mock our efforts
say our battle with the Russian banner
lasted only seven minutes.

3.
They gloat,
> *The White House gates were free of suffrage colors.*
Reporters take sides—
not ours.

4.
Why can't they just report the facts
and let readers decide?

# Picket Day 163
June 21, 1917

The police come to Cameron House
to see Miss Paul.

I listen from the kitchen
with Mrs. Lewis.

> *Stop picketing, or else you'll be arrested,*
> the police chief warns.

*Has the law changed?*
Miss Paul pushes.

> *No, but you must stop it.*

*We have consulted our lawyers.*
*We know we have a legal right*
*to picket.*

> *I warn you,*
> *you will be arrested if you attempt*
> *to picket again.*

They threaten to close
National Woman's Party headquarters.

I sneak out the back door

a coward who is only willing
to dip her toe in
when it's safe.

But when the world comes crashing in
all I want to do is

    run

       far

          away

             where

                no     one

                   will     find me.

## Not the Only One

I wish Joy were here
instead of traveling—
to help untangle me
from this bundle of fear.

Mrs. Lewis finds me.

*Fear is normal,*
she says.

*I don't know if I can keep doing this.*

She cups her hands over mine.
*Every day, I am scared.*
*But I am more scared*
*of what will happen*
*if we don't get the vote.*
*The consequences are too great.*

It helps to know
everyone is a little bit
scared
convincing ourselves to fight
anew
each day.

## Picket Day 164
June 22, 1917

The very next day
police wait outside Cameron House.

Mrs. Morey and Miss Burns
grab banners
head out.

> Go back inside, ma'am,
> a policeman urges.

They walk around him.

> He tries to block
> their
> way.

They carry the president's own words:
> WE SHALL FIGHT FOR THE THINGS
> WHICH WE HAVE ALWAYS CARRIED
> NEAREST OUR HEARTS—
> FOR DEMOCRACY,
> FOR THE RIGHT OF THOSE WHO
> SUBMIT TO AUTHORITY
> TO HAVE A VOICE
> IN THEIR GOVERNMENT.

> Police circle.
> *We have orders to bring you in.*

*On what grounds?*
Miss Burns asks.
*They are the president's own words.*
*We are guaranteed the right to peaceful picketing.*

Miss Paul goes out to confront
the police—
she doesn't hesitate
to challenge authority.

*Little devils!*
The police shout
grab
jerk
tighten handcuffs
arrest them.
They tear Miss Burns's shirt
rough up Mrs. Morey
make them
more wild.

All my worst nightmares
come true.

## Walking Might Save Me

If
I
walk
away
from
Cameron
House
maybe
they
won't
catch
me.
The
police
the
president
the
public
do
not
like
to
see
the
president's
words
on
display.
It
points
out
his
hypocrisy.
All
they

want
is
for
us
to
be
quiet.
But
being
quiet
is
getting
us
nowhere.

## Charges

They are charged:
obstructing traffic.

For standing on a sidewalk.

None
of
this
is
logical.

The judge releases them.

Behind closed doors
they unbutton
and show us
bruises.

# Picket Day 168
June 26, 1917

Six more women
arrested.
The judge expects the accused
to show up to court
a day or two later
to face sentencing.

The charges stick this time.

*Unpatriotic,*
*almost treasonable.*
Accusations fly.

Their choice—
a twenty-five dollar fine
or three days in District Jail
here in the city.

To pay a fine admits guilt—
they are not guilty of obstructing traffic.

Katharine Morey
Annie Arniel
Mabel Vernon
Lavinia Dock
Maud Jamison
Virginia Arnold

Not the first to be arrested
but the first to go to jail.

If Joy were here
she'd be with them.

The more I picket
the more I worry
if I'll be next.


## Walk Away

Sometimes
when I see the police
anger bubbles over.

Even if they aren't coming after me
    if they are just walking on the sidewalk
    if they are laughing
    if they are helping someone.

I have to turn the other direction
walk away
lean against a building
or a gate post
so I can breathe.

When I see the police
fear swallows me.

# We Celebrate
June 28, 1917

Before the women go home
we celebrate our suffrage sisters
in the garden at Cameron House
with breakfast
in honor of them getting out of jail.

Some, like me
face opposition at home—
        a mother who disapproves
        a husband who barely tolerates
        maybe even a son who outright disagrees.

We give them the hero's welcome
they deserve.

# What I Hear about Jail

Inedible food.
Cold cells.
Cockroaches.
Bedbugs.
Rats.
No personal items.

Common criminals
mixed with distinguished women.

The whispers
wind through the women
until we've all heard
what to expect
if we go next.

# Picket Day 174
July 2, 1917

*Why do you picket?*
a congressman asks.
*A penny for your thoughts.*

We do this for you—
the only way to focus attention on suffrage
is to stand here
force you to see us.

*Why don't you go directly to Congress?*
passersby ask from streetcars, buses,
wagons.

We do go to Congress.
They tell us
next session it will be a priority.
Session after session
year after year
nothing changes.

*Why don't you go home,*
*tend your garden?*
another congressman asks.

We tend the garden we want to grow—
where our rights can bloom.

If one more person asks me
WHY
I might shout answers
instead of keeping
quiet.

# A Rare Picnic
July 4, 1917

Father insists we all stay home
for Independence Day
to picnic with the family.
Yesterday's letter from Sophie
broke his heart—
> she's well, but
> he still worries.

I'm grateful to have Joy back
after seven months
still weary from campaigning
for suffrage.

Suffragists plan to picket today.
Independence Day
is only for some citizens.

Yesterday I set out
the banner they carry today.

> GOVERNMENTS DERIVE
> THEIR JUST POWERS
> FROM THE CONSENT
> OF THE GOVERNED.

The city is out celebrating independence—
maybe the police will leave the ladies alone
monitor the drunkards instead.

We lie in the grass
like when we were children.
Father laughs

a gentle, kind laugh that I haven't heard
in a long time.

## Picket Day 176
### July 4, 1917

Joy and I stand
by the White House fence
banners ablaze.

Hazel sells the *Suffragist*
in front of Belasco Theater.

Strangers steal our banners
rip them into shreds.
Hazel goes after them.
A stranger spits on her.
The crowd chases Hazel
until she climbs the fence
holds on
intertwines her arms
locks on.

The police peel her down.
Arrest her
and seventeen others
including Miss Burns
and Joy.

## Consequences of the Right Thing

Each handcuff tightened
each order barked by police
each surge of an angry mob
makes me wince.

My sister
        wrestled into
        the police's Black Maria.

*We are doing the right thing,*
Rose tells me
squeezes my shoulder.
*Especially when it's hard.*

I hold in my tears.

The president looks the other way
sails the Potomac on his yacht
while he sends
husbands and sons and brothers
to Europe
wives and daughters and sisters
to jail.

At least Joy and Miss Burns
will be together.


## The Words that Tumble Out

Mother sees my face
and knows.

*Joy?*
she confirms.

I nod.

                *What happened?*
                Father booms from the doorway.

*Joy's been arrested.*

Father slaps the rolled-up newspaper
onto the table.
*Why can't my girls have quiet jobs?*
*Sell war bonds?*
*Sit and knit like their mother?*
*Be patriotic?*

*Fighting for democracy*
*is patriotic!*
I try to tamp my voice down
but I explode.
*It's what Wilson wants*
*for other countries.*
*Why not ours?*

I don't want to have this fight.
I don't want to say what's burning inside me.
I just want to go lie down
sleep it all off.
*Why can't we have men in our lives*
*who support us?*
The words slip out
and I don't wish them back.

*What are you talking about?*
He waves me off.
*I've stopped complaining about you*
*being suffragettes,*
*but getting arrested?*
*It will ruin your reputations.*

*Suffragists,*
I whisper.

Then I burst,
*Why are you and Arthur against us?*

*Why can't the women*
*in your life*
*have a voice?*

He just stands there
in shock.

## Knitting Is Allowed
July 7, 1917

I dress up to attend court
with the eighteen arrested.

The women sit in front of the judge.
My mind races with worries
about Hazel and Joy
what they'll face in jail.

*On June 21,*
*picketing was legal,*
Miss Burns begins.
*Has the law changed since then?*
*Is it now*
*illegal to picket?*

What is legal?
What is illegal?
The police don't seem to know.
They take it out on the pickets.

The judge takes one look at Hazel
so young among our stoic leaders
dismisses her case outright.
We all exhale in relief.

Joy is so exhausted
she faints.
Will she be another Inez?

The judge grants her mercy
and does not send her to jail.
Joy needs to be forced to rest.

He begs them to pay the fine—
even offers to loan them the money.
They'll have none of it.

Helena Weed asks
if they can knit sweaters in jail
for the war effort.
They aren't menacing criminals
just nice ladies who want to vote.

*Knit all you want to,*
the judge says.
*I don't ask you to stop marching entirely,*
*I only ask you to keep away from the White House.*
*You know the times are abnormal now.*
*We are at war,*
*and you should not bother the president.*

Bother the president?
It should bother him
that boys are in Europe dying
while he is out playing golf.

It should bother him
that women don't have the vote.

## Three Days

For refusing to pay
twenty-five dollars in fines
they spend three days
in jail.

Joy gets three days
of rest—
only because everyone
insists.


## Repercussions

Miss Paul's kidneys aren't functioning—
Bright's disease, the same illness
that killed the president's first wife.
We      all      hold      our      breath.

Miss Paul and Miss Burns
plan for the ultimate victory.

            What will happen
            if Miss Paul dies?

I must put it out of my mind.
I think too much about
the worst possibilities since
Inez.

Miss Burns steps up
as chairwoman
organizes all the girls
while picketing herself.

Worry washes over all of us
but we press on.

## Picket Day 186
July 14, 1917

France celebrates a national holiday—
Bastille Day.
Do our soldiers in France
get a break?
Does the war stop for anything?

I pick up the Bastille Day banners
from the warehouse
with the French motto:

LIBERTY, EQUALITY, FRATERNITY

I'm scheduled to march this afternoon.
Heat grips the city
before the morning pickets begin at ten.

The first group
marches onto the Avenue.
Crowds swarm.

Police grab the pickets
arrest them
push them into a waiting wagon.

A second group goes out
knowing what awaits them.
At the upper gates
police arrest them.

The third group stands
four
long
minutes
before police pile them into vehicles.

Sixteen women
arrested.

When it is my turn to go out
we are out of banners—
they've all been seized.


## Who Holds the Power?

Those of us with afternoon shifts
go to the courthouse with our friends.

Inside the summer-baked courtroom
the women sit on stiff wooden benches
plead their case.

A full room
only lets me squeeze in the back.

Some of them speak out.
*It has been a ridiculous farce*
*for three days!*

But Judge Mullowny
isn't used to ladies talking to him
in this manner.
*Here I have shown you ladies*
*every consideration*
*and have gone out of my way to be patient*

*and you announce it has been a farce.*
*I am astounded.*

Another picket pipes up,
*I know very well*
*we are going to be convicted.*
*We have brought our bags,*
*ready and packed*
*for jail.*

They were prepared for this very moment.
They knew—
and went out anyway.

*The President of the United States*
*who has the power*
*to start in motion*
*the machinery*
*which will give women suffrage*
*and does not do so.*

We all applaud.

A bailiff yells,
*Stop that!*
*Silence!*

The judge calls the room to order.
*If there is any more applause*
*at all in this court,*
*I will order every person*
*except the defendants*
*to be removed.*
*I will not have this for a moment.*

The judge turns red.
His gavel shakes.

Our ladies press on.
*Even when we abide*
*by the law*
*we are punished.*

*The words on your banner*
*are treasonable*
*and seditious.*

France's motto
is treasonous?
France is our ally.
Or is the judge punishing
them for past banners?

I never understand
what they are really being arrested for—
      Violating the White House space?
      Picketing?
      Words on the banner?
This time they claim it is "unlawful assembly."

Or is it really that we are
women with opinions?

Doris Stevens stands to speak:
*The women here*
*have distinguished ancestry:*
*signers of the Declaration of Independence,*
*jurists,*
*Senators,*
*Ambassadors.*

*They look down in spirit*
*upon the trial of women*
*for a declaration of their rights.*

*As long as women*
*go to jail*
*for petty offenses*
*to secure freedom*
*for the women of America,*
*then we will continue*
*to go to jail.*
*Wherever efforts for*
*liberty have been persecuted*
*liberty has in the end*
*prevailed.*

The judge ignores her.
*You are sentenced to sixty days*
*in the workhouse in default*
*of payment*
*of twenty-five dollars each.*

I want to shout,
*The workhouse?*
*Sixty days?*

Even though the words rage inside
no sound comes out.

## Another Option
Even though a judge
prefers they pay a fine

they refuse.

Even though our lawyer
counsels them to pay the fine

they refuse.

Even though I have money
tucked away and offered it

they refuse.

Paying a fine admits wrongdoing.

They

choose

jail.

## Railroaded

They stuff our friends
in railroad cars at Union Station
like cattle carted off
to Virginia
to Occoquan—
where Washington sends some of its prisoners
to work as punishment
thirty miles away
across the river—
a prison for vagrants
drunkards
prostitutes.
I sneak pencils and paper into their bags
to send details to us outside.

# Rumors

**1.**
*Hearsay,*
my mother says,
*is not worth hearing.*

**2.**
Rumors buzz around like flies
at Cameron House.
We know what District Jail is like
but not Occoquan.

**3.**
I hear the food at Occoquan
is worm-infested
not fit for livestock.

**4.**
I hear the Occoquan sheets
crawl with bugs
leftover from the last girl off the street.

**5.**
I hear the farm
where prisoners work
is a farce—
there are still jail cells.

**6.**
I hear Mother and Joy
whispering
about me.
Many of our picketers
have survived jail
but they both worry
what might happen

if I picket
on the wrong day.

7.
My own mother
and sister
don't believe
I'm strong
enough.

## She Holds Me Back

Miss Burns is going to Occoquan to visit
to check on our suffragists
to see for herself if they're okay.

I beg to come along
assist
see what jail is really like.

*No,*
she says.
*Not yet.*

For the first time
she holds me back.

## Forward

Every time I plan to picket
I cannot
sleep.
I overthink
plan every scenario.
If it were not so late,
I'd walk it off.

I reach behind my head
pull out one of Sophie's slips
hold it close to my eyes
to read:

*Sometimes you must be still to move forward.*

I put it in my coat pocket
to remind me
when I want to walk off the picket line
when I'm frustrated with the stillness of protest.

## Picket Day 189
July 17, 1917

Women selling war bonds
watch me
carry the banners to Cameron House.
They whisper—
probably about how I'm not patriotic
enough.

I busy myself with mail
waiting on others to arrive.
I sort them—

> complaints
> support
> inquiries
> information.

I pass out banners
set aside the banner
with the harshest words
for myself.

## Will Today Be the Day?

I follow the experienced
ladies outside.
Rose squeezes my hand
as we cross the Avenue
to the White House gates.

The words will stoke
hatred.

MR. PRESIDENT,
IT IS UNJUST
TO DENY WOMEN
A VOICE IN THEIR GOVERNMENT
WHEN THE GOVERNMENT
IS CONSCRIPTING
THEIR SONS.

I rub the note from Sophie:
*Sometimes you must be still
to move forward.*

I stand
even when I want to

R  U  N.

## Survival

I tend to my blistered feet.
Miss Burns offers bandages
shows me how to wrap them.
*Thank you, Miss Burns.*

*Call me Lucy.*
She smiles.

*Thank you, Lucy.*
Are we friends now?

Lucy seems
worn
from the extra work
while Miss Paul recovers.

Then she tells us about the ladies at Occoquan—
haggard
hungry
existing
lasting.

A few days in the workhouse
changed them.

The matron took their jewelry,
clothing, money, toilet items.
They look like other law-breakers
in their scratchy jail smocks.

They get to come out
to see their lawyer
to see their husbands.

Mr. Hopkins
didn't even recognize
his own wife, Alison,
standing in front of him
dirty
staggering
gaunt
marred
by the brief time
locked away.

# The Effects of Stillness

I
walk
home
raw
skin
scrubbing
the
inside
of
my
shoes.
I
am
not
used
to
standing
in
the
heat.
The
stillness
makes
my
mind
race
takes
my
mind
off
the
pain.
Women
in
Congress!

Women
judges!
A
woman
president!
Do
I
dare
dream?

## Over the Wires
July 18, 1917

We've encouraged women
across the country
to make their voices heard.

A flood of telegrams
wired to the White House
comes in from allies around the country—
angered at the arrests.
They lash out at the president
reprimands on paper
for allowing nice women
to be treated as common thieves.

Do they lie unread
shrapnel scattered
in a fierce battle?

Friends across the country claim to be
appalled
outraged

stunned
that our government
created this injustice—
perpetuates this injustice.

Then why don't they
do something
more than write letters?

## An Offer
The flood of telegrams
pushes the president
to offer a pardon—
a quick release from prison.

Forgiveness.

*But they've done nothing wrong!*
My thoughts
escape my body.
*Pardon admits wrongdoing.*

Some suffragists agree with me
don't blink an eye
when I speak up
like they've
                been
                        waiting for it.

One says,
*A pardon offers escape
from the worms, bedbugs,
filth, terror.*

Mr. Malone offers
the pardon to the women jailed.

*No,*
they say.
*We don't want it.*

## Pardoned
Mr. Malone finally convinces them
to take the pardon.

These women are my heroes—
all sixteen of them—
even if they feel defeated.

On the outside
they can exert more power over Congress.

But first they need a bath
rest
a hot meal.

## Return
July 21, 1917

The jailed ladies return to Cameron House
beleaguered
exhausted
relieved
more determined than ever.

Without hesitation
Mrs. Hopkins

picks up a newly painted banner—
one made at her request.

*Someone else can go out,*
I tell her.
*You must be exhausted.*

*I have to do this,*
she says.
She looks me straight in the eyes
a fire burning within.
She stomps out to show the president—
her husband's friend—
where she stands.

WE ASK NOT
PARDON FOR OURSELVES
BUT JUSTICE FOR ALL
AMERICAN WOMEN.

No police come to arrest her.
But the president himself rides by
salutes.
Does he recognize her?
Does he think
this is over
and forgiven?

# Finally, a Reprieve
July 22, 1917

Word has come from Miss Paul.
She's not dying.
It's not Bright's disease.
Just exhaustion.
Exhaustion
to the point of collapse.
She'll go home to New Jersey
for more rest.

But
she
will
live.

# Picket Day 209
August 6, 1917

The police keep their promises.
They come after the pickets—
all twenty-six of them:

arrest after
arrest after
arrest after
arrest after
arrest after
arrest after
arrest after
arrest after
arrest after
arrest after
arrest after
arrest after
arrest after
arrest after
arrest after
arrest after
arrest after
arrest after
arrest after
arrest after
arrest after
arrest after
arrest after
arrest after
arrest after
arrest.

## Some Days Nothing Happens

My hands callous
from gripping the poles.
My toes blister—
formed over and over
in worn-out shoes.
My face pinks
from standing in the sun.

No one will ever admit
some days, standing
just feels routine.
I will admit
(not out loud)
sometimes it's
boring.

## Picket Day 217

August 14, 1917

Our banners today
will anger others.
Instead of avoiding the one with harsh words
they all want it.

KAISER WILSON,
HAVE YOU FORGOTTEN
YOUR SYMPATHY WITH
THE POOR GERMANS
BECAUSE THEY WERE NOT
SELF-GOVERNED?

20,000,000 AMERICAN WOMEN
ARE NOT SELF-GOVERNED.

TAKE THE BEAM
OUT OF YOUR OWN EYE.

Navy men see it
seethe
yell.

*Grab it!*
someone in the crowd screams.

A sailor tears the banner
off its staff—
rips
shreds
stomps
until it lies in pieces on the sidewalk
leaving us empty-handed
shaken.

The crowd cheers.

## Confrontation
At dinner
Father says grace
before he cuts into his potato.

> *I heard there was a heinous banner*
> *at the picket line today.*

I finally speak up.
*We can't want democracy elsewhere*
*if we don't have it here.*

No one moves.

Father clears his throat.
*I'm not opposed to woman suffrage.*
*I'm opposed to your methods.*

*It got your attention,*
*didn't it?*
*We need people to pay attention—*
*to care about suffrage.*

I get up from the table
without eating
and walk outside.


## A Breath of Fresh Air

Peter is outside
talking to another neighbor.

He can tell by looking at me
I'm not okay.
*Can I get you something?*

*No, I just need a moment.*

He sits down on the stoop
beside me.

*I know you've been out with the suffragists,*
*and I want you to know,*
*I believe in your fight.*

*Thank you.*
*I wish Father believed in us.*

*He'll come around,*
Peter says.

Even if Peter never marches
for suffrage
at least I know
he doesn't waffle
between approval and disapproval.

## Navy Men Don't Stay Away
August 16, 1917

Miss Paul is back.
Fragile
but ready
to take up her banner again.
Lucy tries to talk her out of marching.
She waves her off.

At four o'clock
pickets get ready to face the crowd
when everyone gets off work.

A rumor heard on the street said
the secretary of the navy warned his men
to stay away from the demonstrators.

Lucy tells us,
*Take as many banners as you want.*
*Stuff them up your skirts.*

The navy men are out
watching, taunting.

I grab the last banner.
Someone screams.

The Kaiser banner is in Lucy's grip—
a sailor
pulls it to the ground
drags her mercilessly across the curb.

*Stop!*
But no one can hear me
above the mob.

*Stop!*
Even police stand back
and watch.

## They Stop at Nothing

Lucy escapes—
banners at her chest.

She runs into Cameron House
to the second-floor balcony.

Sailors swarm Cameron House.
They'll break the windows
or the door.

Screams echo throughout the house.

                              Maybe they are mine.

Lucy drapes banners off the balcony—
our private property
not public space.

One sailor puts a ladder against the balcony
and climbs up
          (trespassing)

yanks down the American flag
tears down the banners
throws them to the crowd
          (destruction of private property)

jerks on Lucy's arm
          (assault).

We scream our prayers
as Lucy pulls away.

If he hoists her
over the ledge
she'll fall to her death
          (manslaughter).

It doesn't stop the crowd.
Tomatoes
eggs
hit the windows.
Curses and insults fly like bullets.

When we hear a real bullet
hit a window
we huddle in a corner.

Only then do the police

finally

act.

## Shaken

Rattled.
Cameron House defiled.
Banners tattered.
We crouch away from the windows.
Strong, brave Lucy
crumples.

As the ladies come back in, I see
much more happened out on the street—
blouses ripped
some beaten
others dragged along the sidewalk.

Miss Paul
has tears in her clothes
a gash at her neck.

I take inventory:
148 banners destroyed
or stolen today.
Six dollars each.

Six of our women
arrested.

Were any of the navy men arrested?

We retreat inside Cameron House
wrap our friends in blankets
dab at angry tears.

## All I Can Do

I offer cool cloths
cold water

a place to sit.
Some accept.
Others stare
glassy-eyed
into the distance—
            no outbursts.
Only
silence.


## What Is Easy
August 23, 1917

We have ladies still in jail—
injured from the attack.
We need new banners
but we have empty coffers.
My mind lingers on the horror
of the mob attack.

I busy myself with mail
hope money will fall out of envelopes.

Another executive board member resigns
leaving when the fight is hard
because she says we've gone too far.
Another letter calls us fanatics
seeking notoriety instead of suffrage.

Calmer
kinder
more patient methods
have not given us the vote.

Our methods
keep us in the paper

keep people talking
keep suffrage in legislators' minds.

It is easy for our critics
to quibble over methods
from several states away
while we face
exhaustion
arrests
courtrooms
jail
abuse.

Over and over again.

## Another Suffragist

One night at dinner, Joy tells us she's in love
with Merrill Rogers—
the antiwar magazine man
from New York.

Her frequent trips to New York
aren't just
for suffrage.

*He believes in my work,*
Joy says.
*He believes in our work.*

Father and Mother exchange looks
Mother says,
*We look forward to meeting him.*

## Joy and Merrill

Merrill arrives from New York by train.

Rachel sets an extra plate at the table
in Sophie's spot.

Mother serves stew
and after the first introductions
all I hear is slurping.

Rachel bravely
breaks            the            ice:
*Merrill, tell us about yourself.*

Every eye
focuses on Merrill.

He sits up a little taller
sells himself to us—

*I'm so amazed by Joy
and how tirelessly she works
for the cause.*

Joy blushes.

                    *What do you do, Merrill?*
                    Father asks a question
                    he knows the answer to.

*I work in New York,
for a magazine.*

He leaves out the part about it being
antiwar.

Joy probably warned him
ahead of time.

He asks polite questions of each of us
blends in with our boisterous dinner table.
Father and Arthur do one thing right—
neither starts a fight about politics.

## Arrested Again
August 28, 1917

Lucy is arrested—
whisked off to Occoquan
again.
They think
if they jail her
every time
we will stop
picketing
without our leader.
She wants us to continue
without her.
And we do.

## The Cost of Being in Jail
September 13, 1917

News comes in to Cameron House daily—
letters, telegrams, phone calls.
But when we get the news
that Lucy is in solitary
at Occoquan
the buzz of sorting and typing
stops.

The imprisoned women drafted a letter
demanding to be treated as political prisoners
passed it down the pipes from cell to cell.
Political prisoners
are supposed to have more rights
unlike common criminals.

We hear that the warden is threatening,
*We are going to stop your picketing.*
*If it costs the lives of some of your women,*
*we will stop it.*

The typewriters start again—
rage
turned into
action
keeps us going
on days of despair.

## Picket Day 270
### October 6, 1917

1.

On a mild fall day
the sun is thin upon the Avenue.
Our purples, whites, golds
flutter in the wind.
Our banners ask the president
again
what he'll do for suffrage.

2.

Congress is in its last days
of an Emergency War Session
but they still

will not consider
our right to vote.

3.
Joy, Rose, and I
carry our banners
toward the crowd
already anticipating
our arrival.
I'm no longer nervous.
After a few months this feels
normal.

4.
Women and men
watch and wait
for us.
We speak with our words.
They stand in our silence
read our banners.

5.
One sailor
targets me.
Banner ripping from the pole
he throws it onto the sidewalk
stomps his feet
tramples it.

6.
The crowd taunts.
Every word
I want to say
gets caught in my throat.
My heart races.

7.
When the sailor runs off
I pick up
the crumpled banner
smooth it out
fasten it back
to the pole
stay standing.

8.
The police come swiftly
jerk my arms behind my back—
pull at my shoulders
even though I don't resist.
The cold metal
of handcuffs
tightens around me
constrains me.
I try to breathe.

9.
One by one
they push
into the Black Maria.
I am smashed between
Joy and Rose
stoic guards on either side
to protect me.

10.
Once we are alone
in the back
others smile
my heart beats out of my chest.

# What People Think of Me

I don't think about
what Father or Arthur will say about my arrest.

I don't think about
what the judge's sentence will be.

I don't think about
what the warden will do to me.

I don't think about
what crowds on the street think of me.

My only thought is—
am I strong enough for jail?


# Punishment

The police release me
to Father
who takes me home
in silence.

My arrest
warrants a peek at a note from Sophie.
I count
only
three
left.
So I save them.

I find an old quote from Sophie
tucked away in a drawer,
just the one I need.

*An unjust punishment can garner attention.*

## How to Be a Good Citizen

Support the president—
      even when you disagree with him.
Support the president—
      even when he ignores his own citizens.
Support the president—
      even when
      you can't vote.


I am not a good citizen.


## What to Do with Us

October 8, 1917

Two days later
I'm in court
awaiting my own fate.

Any demands from the court
are met
with our silence.
Talk gets us nowhere.

An army of women sits behind me.
I can't keep my hands from shaking.

They try to swear me in.
      I refuse.
They ask me questions.
      I am silent.
They ask my age.
      I am stoic.

Miss Paul speaks for us,
*As an unenfranchised class,*

*we have nothing to do with the making*
*of the laws which have put us in this position.*
*How can we be held at a court*
*that doesn't recognize our rights?*
*Or be punished by a government*
*that doesn't allow us to participate?*

The judge
too familiar with our work
doesn't know what to do with us
doesn't know how to answer Miss Paul
so he doesn't sentence us.

We are at the mercy
of his moods.

We go home
for now.

I finally exhale.

## We Talk of Marriage

Father and Arthur are waiting
at the kitchen table
food untouched.
Father's eyes widen
when we walk in
surprised and relieved.

*We were not sentenced,*
Joy says.

> *You're very lucky.*
> Father takes off his glasses.

*You knew this would happen,*
Arthur says at me.
*You'd get arrested eventually.*
*No one will want to marry a girl*
*who's been arrested—*

I know their argument
is precisely untrue.
*Joy's been arrested more than I have—*
*and Merrill knows it.*

Joy nods.

*What if I don't want to get married?*
It was the first time I'd said the words aloud.

Father furrows his brow
sticks out his lips.
*Not many men are like Merrill,*
*willing to take on a feisty,*
*strongheaded troublemaker.*

*I'm*
*not*
*looking*
*for*
*a*
*husband.*
I know they can hear me.
Do they not believe me?

*One day,*
*you might want a husband,*
*so you'll need to change your ways.*
Unmarried Arthur gives me advice.
He told me to speak up.

Now I'm better off
silent.

*You*
*are*
*not*
*listening.*

Rachel bursts through the front door
a stack of papers in her hands.
*What happened?*

> *Apparently, they aren't going to jail,*
> Arthur says,
> thoroughly disappointed.

After Arthur leaves
Joy says,
*It's not true, you know.*
*Someone will want to marry you.*

*If I have the vote,*
*and I have a job,*
*and I have my own place,*
*I won't need a husband.*

*I never wanted one either,*
Joy says,
*until I met Merrill.*

Just because we're sisters
doesn't make me want the same things.

# Picket Day 284
October 20, 1917

Each day on the picket line
we don't know if it will be quiet
or crowded.
Each day I prepare the banners
before the pickets arrive.
I keep an eye out for shift changes
ready to step in
if a spot needs to be filled.

Today Miss Paul and Rose
picket together
using the president's own slogan
for Liberty Bonds:

THE TIME HAS COME
TO CONQUER OR SUBMIT.
FOR THERE IS BUT
ONE CHOICE—
WE HAVE MADE IT.

Seven of our suffragists
are carried away in a police van.
Why do the president's own words
get our ladies arrested?

But the judge
is tired of seeing us.
Miss Paul gets seven months
in the District Jail—
the longest sentence yet.

They continue to think if they put away
our ringleader
we'll stop picketing.

They haven't learned yet.

## Begging
October 23, 1917

While Miss Paul and Rose and others
languish in jail
Lucy writes letters to supporters
begging for one-dollar donations
to replenish our depleted funds.
I stuff envelopes
address them
mail them.

Small donations multiplied
will make a difference.
Lucy is not afraid to beg.

## Rumors of District Jail
November 6, 1917

We hear
about the large rats
strong enough to move chairs.

We hear
Rose and Miss Paul are tireless with song
while other inmates beg to sleep.

We hear
they're treated worse than murderers.

We hear
they've decided on a hunger strike.

## Strength
Rose keeps in touch through notes:

*All the officers here know we are making this hunger strike,*
*that women fighting for liberty may be considered political prisoners;*
*we have told them.*
*God knows we don't want other women ever*
*to have to do this again.*

The warden force-feeds
Rose and Miss Paul
shoves tubes
down their throats
pours milk and eggs

d

o

w

n

gagging them
until they vomit.

They endure this torture
three times a day.

I worry about their health
their exhaustion.
How can we ensure they'll survive this?
Our struggle is offering strength
from the outside.

Maybe there are some things
we must each endure
alone.

## How Can We Celebrate Now?

It's odd that devastating news
and thrilling news
arrive together.

My stomach is in knots with worry over Rose
while today we hear
New York women
got the vote!

We must celebrate
every victory
but my mind keeps wandering to Rose—
a tube gagging her
as she fights for women
who still don't have
the choice
the freedom
of enfranchisement.

## Joy Tells All
November 8, 1917

Joy travels to Mississippi
on tour for suffrage.

She promises to share
the true story of Sentinels
      sore feet and
      ripped clothes and
      false arrests and
the true story of Occoquan
      worms and
      fleas and
      solitary and
the true story of District Jail
      rats and
      hunger and
      no air.

Once more people know
what's really happening
they will be appalled.

## Picket Day 305
November 10, 1917

Lucy invites members nationwide
to march in protest
of Miss Paul's imprisonment.

But the invitation came
with a warning—
prepare for imprisonment
if you choose to come.

We protest—
forty-one strong.

Putting Miss Paul in jail
only emboldens us.

We form the longest
picket line—
The crowd shouts
their support.
The police arrest all forty-one of us.

I don't think I'll ever get used to
the cold metal
clamping
around my wrists—
the uncertainty of what comes after
the whims of a judge
who decides my fate.

Maybe a judge
will put us in jail
with Miss Paul.

They could fill up
the District Jail
with murderers
and suffragists.

## Inoculation
November 11, 1917

They don't sentence us right away
or lock us up.

We go back out
circle the District Jail.
Suffragists outnumber guards.
We push through—
they move out of our way.

*Miss Paul!*
we yell,
*Alice Paul!*

She's in there
likely dying
from her hunger strike.
When her face appears in an upstairs window
we rejoice.
Her fingers reach out
yet we do not connect.
We tell her of our fate—
jail for us tomorrow.

*Prepare for intolerable conditions,*
she warns.
*Insist on being political prisoners*
*from the beginning.*

A rush of guards
ushers us away
clamps the handcuffs on us
again.

But we have what we need—
inoculation from our leader
preparing and protecting us
for what lies ahead.

## Last Walk in Freedom

I
walk
home
to
tell
my
parents
I'm
about
to
face
sentencing.
They
knew
this
was
coming.
Judges
don't
dismiss
charges
anymore—
to
prove
a
point.
It
doesn't
work.
I
pull
the
fresh
air
into

me
before
jail
air
can
take
over.

# WHATEVER THE COST

## COST

Mid-November–December 1917

## I Pack My Bags

I have no one to ask
what I'll need in jail.

I pack my bag
with toiletries
Votes for Women sash
books to read and paper
extra clothing.

We can't keep our own things in jail
but the ladies always try—
part of their demands as political prisoners.

Father doesn't say anything at first.
He doesn't seem angry
just resigned.
*We'll miss you,*
he says as I leave.
*This house keeps getting quieter.*

He reaches out his arms
and I bury my tears
in the folds of his shirt.

## My Sentence

Mother is on a hard wooden bench
in the courthouse
when the judge
sentences me to only fifteen days
because I'm the youngest at nineteen.

I think I hear Mother cry out
but when I turn around
she is stoic.

The judge sentences others—
two women get fifteen days for their first offenses
twenty-nine women get thirty days.

Lucy gets
SIX
months.

All of us are headed to Occoquan—
the filthy workhouse
where food crawls with worms.
The faraway workhouse
in the Virginia woods
where those on the outside
will never know
what they do to us.

Some women I don't know—
out-of-towners
who picketed on an unlucky day.
But Mrs. Lewis
and Lucy
will be there.
At least I will have friends
my first time in prison.

## Instructions

Before we leave
the courthouse

Lucy gathers us all together
in a tight circle.

*When we get to the workhouse,*
*do not speak.*
*If they ask for your name,*
*stay silent.*
*Resist,*
*but resist without talking.*
*Just like at the White House gates.*
*Silence.*
*I will make the demands.*

My tongue goes dry
like swallowing rocks.

What will we need to resist?

## Worry

We cram into a train car
tight enough to feel the tickle of hair
from the woman next to us.

Silence snakes through the car
until only the rock of the train
envelops us.

Worry slithers in
shaking my hands.

Every clack of the track
jostles questions around in my mind.

What     is          to          come?

Will        we        be        hurt?

Will

I

survive?

## Premonition
The jailers at Occoquan
will confiscate our bags
so I take one last peek
only to find a Hershey's Kiss
from Father
and my last three Sophie notes
on top—

> *Thought you might need these.*
> *Stay safe!*
> *—Rachel*

Inside one note
she tucked a tiny pencil.
I hide them in my undergarments.

I slip the chocolate kiss into my mouth—
a last moment of bliss
and my first act of resistance.


## Demands
The journey isn't long
but dread makes me weary.
We arrive at six thirty
and the warden can't be found.

We must see the warden
to ask to be treated as political prisoners.

Lucy makes demands
presses the matron,
*Let us see Warden Whittaker!*
Lucy has met him before.

Matron Herndon,
a stern-faced jailer,
tells us we'll be waiting
all night.
Maybe longer.
*Give me your names,*
she demands.

I press my lips together.
Not a single name escapes
from the mouths of our group.

Sometimes there is safety
in silence.

Sometimes
silence ignites.

*No more begging for the warden,*
one guard growls.

*May I use the lavatory?*
I ask
finally breaking my silence.
*May I have some water?*
Mrs. Lewis begs.

*No*
*no*
*no!*

The noes come sharp
swift.

The matron's voice rattles
as she asks for our names
again.

*We demand to be treated*
*as political prisoners.*
Mrs. Lewis is resolute.
She borrows Lucy's line.
She is the oldest
and she has had enough.

*We don't recognize political prisoners,*
the matron says.
*You are just like all of the other*
*criminals here.*
*I'll collect your things,*
*then you can be off to your cells.*

## Jailbird

I'm nineteen
and in jail—
a criminal
still awaiting a place to lay my head
for the night.

I hear a familiar voice
through the thin walls.

Mother.

I saw her face in court
only a few hours ago—
how did she reach me so quickly?

She pleads.
A guard gives gruff answers.

I scream,
*Motherrrrr!*
*Motherrrrr!*
*M—*
A guard rushes to me
raises a hand.
I cower
close my eyes
wait for the blow.

*You can't see your mother.*
*She'll be sent away.*

Mrs. Lewis argues.
*She's just a girl.*
*Let her mother take her home.*

The guard looks at her with evil eyes
then walks away.
I gasp for air.
Tears escape
without permission.

Mrs. Lewis puts her hand
in mine.

## Respect for the Elderly

Warden Whittaker storms in like a tornado.
His stiff white hair
and blazing little eyes
terrify.

*You shut up!*
He points at Mrs. Lewis.
*I have a man here glad to handle you!*
*Seize her!*

Not Mrs. Lewis!
She's old
frail.
They might break her bones.

They do not
care.

They          d     r     a     g
Mrs. Lewis—
her bad foot

        d
          a
           n
            g
              l
                e
                  s
                      l
                      i
                      m
                      p.

They throw her onto a bed with no mattress.

# SLAM

her against iron rails

a       g       o       n       y

all over her face.

Shedoesnotmove.

Is she

dead?

*Mrs. Lewis!*
My screams
echo off the walls.
I grab on to the bars
pull at them
but they don't budge.
I scream,
*Mrs. Lewwwwwiiiiiisssssss!*

She finally groans.
She's alive.

A guard
laughs.

I curl into a ball
free myself to take the next necessary
breath.

## Unprepared

I've always wanted
my own space
my own room.
Here I am alone.

Nothing could have prepared me for
this
empty
cell.
This
fear.

Nothing.

## Roll Call

We refuse roll call
for Matron Herndon
but not for Lucy.

She calls out to us from her cell—

*Mrs. Nolan?*

*I am here.*

*Mrs. Cosu?*
*Mrs. Lewis?*
*Are you okay?*

The guards seize Lucy
for checking on us
her legs scissoring.
The guards struggle.

*Lucy!*
I scream.

Warden Whittaker grabs her from the guards
threatens to shove horse bits
in her mouth
to silence her.

He must not know anything
about her.

She will not be silenced.

## Alone

My thoughts are trapped in my head
like I am in this tiny cell.
They circle around and around
worries returning
spiraling out of control.

If they'll throw an old lady
against an iron bed frame
what else will they do
to her?
To me?

The mattress is a board.
My teeth chatter
from the cold
until I can no longer think
of anything
except being warm.

I could
beg for a pardon

beg to go home
beg for Father to pay my fine.
Any groveling necessary to get me
out.

But I can't.

I am not a coward.
I can keep going.


## A Reminder

I unroll the first note from Sophie
when the guard turns his back.
We might be in here longer than
three notes' worth
but I might not make it through
tonight
without a reminder.

*You'll never know your strength until you test it.*

Not my strength—
all of us together.
Even in our cold cells
even in our pain
even in our fear
we carry the strength
of suffragists from across the country.


## The Guards vs. Lucy

*We've never been treated
this way before,*
Lucy says to the guards
but loud enough for us to hear.

The guards did as they promised—
handcuffing Lucy.
They wrangle.
She writhes.

*You keep coming back,*
the guard says.
*Each time,*
*it will get worse.*

Her cell is across from mine.
They force her hands above her head.
Her rag-doll body

h
a
n
g
s.

I lock eyes with her
put my hands above my head in

s
o
l
i
d
a
r
i
t
y.

She kicks
fights

until
the fight drains out.
Can she breathe?
Hanging there like that?

Silence.
Stillness.

I drop my hands
grip the cell door.

*Lucy?*

There is no movement.
There is no noise.

*Nooooo!*
I scream.
*Luuuuuuuuuuucccccccccyyyyyyyyyyyyyy!*

Others scream from their cells.
Our echoes
haunt the halls.


## Silent No More

I scream for hours
calling out
using my voice
until it's hoarse.

The guards wince
when I scream.
The warden rages
when I scream.

So I

SSSSCCCCRREEEAAAAAAAAAAMMMMMMM

from my cell
until my voice
is
gone.

## This Night Won't End
The guards aren't done.
I crane to see
but I can only hear.

A
            thud.

They throw one of our ladies
like a sack of potatoes
across her cell.
She whimpers
after they leave.

They whisk Mrs. Nolan away—
to see a doctor,
they say.
Her foot
her heart
all need attending.

Mrs. Cosu cries out in pain
clutches her arm
struggles to breathe.
Something is wrong with her heart.

I can't reach her—
but I smell the vomit.
She wretches continuously.
This will surely kill her.

*Mrs. Cosu,*
*are you all right?*
I whisper to her
but she cannot speak.

Lucy's raspy voice
barely whispers
to us.
*I.*
*Can't.*
*Feel.*
*My.*
*Fingers.*

*Let Miss Burns down!*
I urge the guards.
*She can't breathe!*

The guards remain still.

*Help Mrs. Cosu!*
*Something's terribly wrong.*

The guards walk
away.

I crumple.
My angry tears
wet the ground.

# Will They Give Up?

Cold creeps in
wafts through the cells.

Boots
echo down the corridor.

Shallow breaths
come lighter, slower.

The fight
given up.

Bodies
can no longer persist.

Silence.

## How to Survive Jail

I sit
alone
in my cell
shivering.
The thin drape
issued by the jail
doesn't warm me.

If Joy were here
maybe
she would know how to survive this.

I have fifteen days.
I mark time
on my cell wall
with a nub of a pencil hidden in Sophie's notes.
|

Fourteen more to go.

# Walk in a Jail Cell

There's not much space to pace in this cell, but I must walk to think. Thoughts jumble together, interrupted by screams, I try to breathe, but the stench overpowers me. I don't want to die in here. I know we have to play this game, us vs. them, and they cannot win. We must be strong, summon strength from places we did not know we had. We have to help each other hold on. We cannot allow them satisfaction from our torture, no joy from our tears, no pleasure from our pain. We are strong. So I will remind them.

## Unlocked

After many long hours
a kind guard
unlocks Lucy's handcuffs.

She thumps to the floor

crumpled.

For a few long seconds
she is still.

When she finally moves
we breathe
again.


## In the Darkness

I lie awake
wishing for a blanket
and a sister nearby.
I wish for sleep
to carry me away.

The boots stomping
in the hallway
the laughter
from the guards
keeps me from drifting off.

Whimpers come from other cells.
No one sleeps
for fear we might not wake.

# The Longest Night

I unroll another note from Sophie
in the dark
squinting.

*It's only in the dark that we appreciate the light.*

I pray morning comes
quickly.

# II

## The Next Morning
we are all still alive.
I make another tally

of hope—
that we make it through the whole day.

They leave food for us in our cells
as if last night never happened.

I hear from cell to cell
that Lucy and Mrs. Lewis
will hunger strike
like Rose and Miss Paul
in the District Jail.

Flies swarm the uneaten food
even in cold November.

They cannot force me to eat.
I cannot stomach the thought.

# III

## The Looks on Other People's Faces

Marines from Quantico
come in to help guard us
keep us in line
but they see the horrors we face.

One of the Marines
contacts our lawyer, Matthew O'Brien.

Mr. O'Brien
works with Mr. Malone.
He demands to see us.
The guards know
he knows
the unspeakable things they've done
to us.

Mr. O'Brien stares.
His face tells me
it's as bad as I think it is.
One by one
he looks at us
shocked
speechless.

## Stench

Even the bitter cold
doesn't tame the stench.
Unflushed toilets
foul the air.
Only the guards can flush the toilets
from outside our cells.

They swing their night sticks
ignore our requests.
What do they tell their wives
when they go home?
We are bound to be in the papers.

Or do they wash off the stench of jail
and not speak of it?

## Hunger

I refuse
milk and toast.

But when they bring
fried chicken
with crispy skin still sizzling
it fills our cells with its warm aroma.
One guard stands in full view
snacking on a chicken leg.

My stomach cramps
desperate to be filled.

A penciled note comes in along the pipes
from Lucy:

> *They think there is nothing in our souls
> above fried chicken.*

## It Hasn't Stopped
I hear Mrs. Lewis
gagging
struggling
against the restraints
of nurses, doctors, the matron.

They take her blood pressure
listen to her heart.
They must keep her alive.

I need her to stay alive.

I stare at the tobacco spit on the floor
wrap myself in a dirty horse blanket
close my eyes.
Remember to
breathe.


## Force-Feeding
The warden says he's tired
of our hunger strike
doesn't want martyrs on his watch.
*Force-feedings begin today,*
he says.
He walks down the cell block
with a rubber tube in his hands.

I hear them
cracking
eggs.

They hoist Mrs. Lewis up first.
We can hear her cries
their voices
echoing.

If I climb up the bars
I can just see
into the next room
five people holding her

d

      o

         w

           n.

Her face is drained of color.
I don't know if her heart can take it.
They thrust the tube down her nose.
Eggs and milk
are poured down the tube
while
she

g      a      s      p      s

for air

gags

on the concoction.

Lucy is next.

Lucy's
blood
spreads

everywhere.
Staining.
Leaving its mark
on her
on the nurses
on the doctor.
But they continue
dumping slop down
her nose
into her stomach.

They haven't come
for the rest of us
yet.

## Refusal

We all hunger strike.

The matron complains.
*The insolent hunger strikers!*

The guards interrogate us
attempt to break our morale.

*You will work!*

                                          *No!*

*You will put on prison clothes!*

                                          *No!*

*You will eat!*

                                          *No!*

*You will not cause trouble!*

                                          *No!*

We want to be unbreakable

        but I'm cracking from the inside.

## ||||| |||

## Footsteps

I've never been hungry
like this.
Pangs eat at my stomach
double me over.
The guards shove dry toast at me.

We are treated like animals
in a pen.

All day I hear footsteps.
I tense with each sound.

## Gone

The next morning
Lucy's cell is empty.

*Lucy?*
I call out.
*Where's Lucy?*

*Mrs. Lewis and Lucy are gone*
*to District Jail,*
a guard says.
*Warden Whittaker doesn't want them to die*
*on his watch.*

We will
continue
without our leaders.

Our bodies
our spirits
are weak
but our minds
are strong.

We need to keep our minds
sharp
as we waste away in these jail cells.
Doing nothing.

Every day we spend in jail
sends a message to the president
to Congress
to women around the country:
we will not quit.

## Holding On

Abandoned—
even though Lucy and Mrs. Lewis
left without choice.

Addled—
overcome with confusion
irrational thoughts
even though I know it's the gnawing hunger.

Angered—
at the abuse of power
at the hands of public servants
who treat us like vermin.

A Sophie note pokes at me—

*In your worst moment, hold fast to what you believe.*

Is this the worst?
Or is there more to come?
I'm not experienced with jail
hunger striking
like Lucy and Miss Paul—
our beacons.

But none of us have relented
or asked to go home.
We hold fast.

## I Wake Up Gasping

I shiver all night.
When I do let myself
succumb to sleep
even a small drip
a mouse scurry
a snore
startles me.
I wake up gagging
trying to pull out a rubber tube
that isn't there
trying to throw up eggs
I never swallowed.

## Beyond the Cells

There are woods
outside these walls.
Matron Herndon offers to take us out
for a walk.
Get fresh air.

## Walking with Matron Herndon

Three
of
us
agree
to
go—
skeptical
of
Matron Herndon.
When
the
scent
of
wet
grass
hits
my
nose
I
want
to
run
into
the
dark
woods
and
hope
it
leads
toward
home.
But
I
walk

deliberately
step
by
step
pace
myself.
We
all
exchange
glances
but
stay
silent.
Matron Herndon
talks
but
I
only
listen
to
crickets
frogs
bloodhounds.

## The Consequences of a Walk

*We must hurry,*
the Matron says.
*The bloodhounds are loose.*

We are dizzy
from the hunger strike.
*Would they attack us?*
I ask.

*They will find us,*
Matron Herndon says.

Hunger confuses us.
She gave us fresh air.
Is that not allowed?

Matron Herndon's face is ashen.
Why did she take this risk?
Maybe she needed
fresh air too.

The searchers get closer.

I can run
even as the world
spins.

## Too Weak to Fight

Matron Herndon grabs us by our collars
as we approach the door.

*I found them,*
she announces.
Her betrayal complete.

The other guards race to help her
as if we could fight them
in our famished state.

I want to rat her out
but I know she'll make things worse
for us
if I expose
her.

# The Lies They Tell Us

*No one is trying to reach you from outside,*
       *they say.*
*Your attorney abandoned your case,*
       *they say.*
*You are the only one hunger striking,*
       *they say.*
*The other women put on prison clothes and are working,*
       *they say.*
*Miss Burns and Mrs. Lewis paid their fines to escape,*
       *they say.*

They try to break me.
They try to convince me no one cares.
I might be hungry
but I know Lucy and Mrs. Lewis.
They are still fighting.

The guards fill me with lies
but I spit them out.

**॥॥ ॥॥॥**

## Temptation

Tomorrow we go to court
so the warden can transfer us
out of his care
I can barely stand.

Will they
carry me
drag me
leave me
on the floor?

They try to feed us again.
Dragging starved women
into court
doesn't look good.

They slip
baked apples
into our cells
as temptation.

The smell of a warm apple
caramelized in its own juices
makes my mouth water
and for a moment
masks the wretched smell
of unflushed toilets.

I lean close
let the apple's steam rise
smell the temptation.

Across the hallway
I watch Kathryn
devour her apple.

I am jealous
of her delight.

||||  ||||

## They See Us

We have court today.
Walking takes extra effort
when you're starving.
My body slumps in need of sleep.

*Hurry up!*
Matron Herndon yells.
*It was your choice to ruin your bodies!*

We walk into the courtroom
gasp
after
gasp
fills the space.

Some of us lie down on the benches
others stare at the judge
hollow          hungry          tired
but alive.
We've survived.

There are whispers
until the judge bangs his gavel.

I feel sick
wishing I'd eaten the baked apple
to fill the gap.

They want to transfer us
to the District Jail

where the others waste away.
But the warden there
doesn't want us.

I want to go home.
I'm tired
of suffrage.

## The Verdict

They claim Lucy is too ill to come to court.
Mr. O'Brien notices and calls it out.
*If three days ago*
*it was necessary to handcuff Miss Burns*
*to the walls of a cell,*
*we consider her well enough to appear.*

We were sentenced to Occoquan
because we were able-bodied—
we could work.
The judge looks over Mrs. Nolan
seventy-three years old
dressed in black
frail
fragile.

The judge orders us out of Occoquan.
I almost smile
until I realize
it's just a different cell
in a different jail.

## The Powerful

The powerful decide
who goes to jail
for how long.

The powerful decide
who is dismissed
to go home.

The powerful decide
how we'll be treated
in jail.

All the more reason
why reasonable women
need to be in power.


## Together Again

They tell me
Rose is here—
weak, but here
in the District Jail.

Lucy is here too
but I haven't seen either one.

Are they ill?
Injured?
Hungry?

We are emaciated
worn
threadbare.

I collapse
from the journey here
pray this is almost over.

Wearenotalone.
Westandtogether.
Ihopewegetoutalive.

卌 卌 III

## My Dreams Become Clear

The tallies
from my last cell
follow me here.

I spend the night
on a cold floor.

The room spins
as I dream
of food
instead of

voting.

HHT HHT IIII

## Freedom

They line us up
for release.

Regardless of our sentence
we will all
be released
today.

I put on my torn Votes for Women sash
fear it's all a cruel joke.

But the door
opens
to fresh air.

*We are political prisoners,*
Lucy tells the warden.

*You are not political prisoners—*
*you are free.*

*We are political prisoners,*
Lucy starts to chant.
We join in.

The warden orders his men to scuttle us out
and lock the jail doors behind us.

We are
released.

## What Next?

I am stiff
dirty.
I want to go home.

Freedom smells like
fresh air
warm coffee
clean bath
a long, long night's sleep.

## They Lied to Mother

Mother waits for me
outside the jail
wraps me in a hug.

*I tried,*
she sobs.
*I tried to come see you.*

*I know,*
*I heard your voice.*

Her pent-up words tumble out.
*They wouldn't let me in.*
*I tried our friend Mr. Tumulty,*
*Mr. Wilson's secretary.*
*I told him you didn't have enough warm clothes.*
*He told me*
*you would have plenty of clothes.*
*He told me*
*the rumors weren't true.*
*He told me*
*you would be safe.*
*He told me*

*they would take good care of you.*
*But I look at you and—*

Mother wails
crumples onto the sidewalk.

*Mother!*
I put my thin arms around her.
*I'm all right.*
*I'm here.*
*I survived.*


## I Return Home
I walk in the door
with Mother's help
barely able to carry my own bag.
The smell of food overwhelms.

Everyone is at the table waiting
trying to busy themselves with work
knitting
reading.

Arthur comes over first
wraps me in a hug so tight
it hurts.
He's shaking
holding back tears.

Father's face looks older.
He wraps his arms
around both of us.

Rachel is gentler with her hugs.
Relief is written on everyone's faces.

They show me a telegram from Joy.

MATILDA TO BE RELEASED.
HOME SOON.
JOY.

An early Thanksgiving feast
is spread all over the kitchen.
I'd wished for food for days
but I can't stomach much.
An entire box of Hershey's Kisses
sits at my spot at the table.
It's not even Sunday.

I fall to the floor
and sob.
Arthur scoops me up
and carries me to my room.

## I'm Okay

Rachel brings clean clothes.
Everyone lets me use
the lavatory
for as long as I want.

She spoons
small sips of broth
into my cracked lips
turns to wipe her own tears.

*I'm okay,*
I tell her.
She holds me
as I sink into her arms.

*I'm okay.*
*I didn't quit,*
I tell her.


## When Sleep Doesn't Come

I can't sleep
even in my warm room
with Rachel beside me.
I tiptoe downstairs
open up Father's newspaper.

My hands shake
my body still struggling
from eating for the first time in days.
My vision blurs as I try
to scan the headlines.

Rachel comes down.
*You okay?*

*Just reading*
*before Father burns the paper in the morning.*
*I wanted to see what they said about us.*

She sits down with me.
I try to close my eyes.
She begins to read the words of the District Jail's warden
a man grateful to be rid of us
left to deal only with real prisoners:
*"Thanksgiving this year,"*
*he said in a voice choked with gratitude,*
*"will be Thanksgiving indeed.*
*The ways of Providence are inscrutable.*
*But I have been given cause*

*to be thankful*
*and I will be thankful as never before."*

Rachel pauses.
I open my eyes to read her face.
She wipes a tear quickly
trying to hide it from me.

*Providence.*
I echo the Warden's words.
*I guess he thinks God's on his side.*
(We must know two different Gods.)

She continues.
At the end of the article

she reads the names of the released prisoners—
including mine.
Tears stream down her face.

She doesn't try to hide them
this time.

## Breathing Exercises

Just
before
sunrise
I
walk—
freedom
smells
like
woodsmoke
rising
from

the
city's
chimneys.
Crisp
late-fall
air
opens
my
lungs.
All
those
days
in
jail
I
tried
to
breathe
lightly
not
wanting
to
taste
the
stench.
But
now
I
can
breathe
deep
fill
my
lungs
intoxicate
myself

with
freedom.
I
still
look
over
my
shoulder.
My
bones
still
ache
but
I
will
walk
until
the
aches
disappear.

## Pinning
December 6, 1917

We've been free
for ten days.

Miss Paul still wears her fur coat
she donned the day she came out of jail
barely walking—
like she hasn't been warm for months.

I attend the NWP Conference
at the Belasco Theater.

They call me
to the stage
pin a silver pin
shaped like a prison cell door
with a heart-shaped lock
on my lapel.

Each of us
jailed for the freedom to vote
wear the pins
as badges of honor.

It becomes the most prized
in my collection.

## Merrill Becomes Part of the Family

December 10, 1917

Joy returns from Tennessee
marries Merrill Rogers
in New York City.
I send best wishes
but I am in no shape to make the trip.

## Too Many Questions

Hazel was always braver than I was
on the picket line.
But she's never gone to jail.

She waits weeks
then breaks the silence.
*What was it really like?*
*The Night of Terror?*
*The hunger strike?*

Her questions bubble up out of her.
They
don't
stop.

I shake my head.
*I can't.*

*Oh, Matilda,*
*I'm sorry.*
*I didn't mean to pry.*
*I just—*
*I'm amazed by you,*
*by Lucy,*
*by the ladies who made it through.*
*I can't imagine.*

*You can't.*

*Are you angry with me?*
*I didn't mean to be cruel.*

*No, I'm not angry.*
*I didn't choose to go through*
*the Night of Terror.*
*I just chose to survive it.*
*I can't talk about it.*
*Not yet.*

## Echoes
Each night
I lie awake.
I am safe
but I can still hear the clomp of the boots
Mrs. Lewis screaming

Lucy gasping for breath
as she hangs in her handcuffs.

My heart races.
I can't calm myself.

I think no one hears me
take one breath
a t    a    t i m e.

I think no one hears me
mumble
*I cannot go to jail again.*
*I cannot go to jail again.*
*Don't make me go to jail*
*again.*

But Rachel must hear
must know.
She puts her arms around me
holds me until I fall asleep.

# AS LONG AS IT TAKES

## TAKES

January 1918–November 1920

## By Day, I Fight

At night
I battle nightmares
but each morning
I am ready to battle any man
that stands in my way—
congressmen
sailors on the street
guards
even the president.
I didn't go to jail to back down.

Today, I ready myself for Capitol Hill.
The president has urged men
to vote for our amendment.

Mother makes sandwiches.
I stuff one in my pocket
kiss her goodbye.

If I live on my own
how will I eat?
If it weren't for her
I'd likely forget.


## When They Hear

Joy and many others
travel the country
telling what happened to us—
         the violence
         the neglect
         the force-feeding
other women
stand in shock.

Hundreds or thousands of miles
from our jail cells
they can't imagine the cruelty.
Money pours in to continue
the fight.
Membership multiplies.
They can't ignore
our plight

      once they know about it.


## Picket Day 366
January 10, 1918

Today is not just any day.
Forty years ago
today
they introduced
Susan B. Anthony's amendment.

One year ago
today
Silent Sentinels
began picketing.

Debate begins
in the House.

Some want to vote on suffrage
today.
Others want to wait
until the war is over.

At five o'clock
debate closes
voting begins.

I lean forward in my seat
my long-gone sandwich
rumbling my stomach.
Who is for us today?
Who is against us?

One congressman
leaves a hospital bed
just to vote
YEA.

Another congressman
arrives ill
with doctor and nurse in tow
to vote
YEA.

When the roll call
comes
the room stills.

They check names carefully
for this close vote.

We wait.

165 Republicans
104 Democrats
vote for us
today
for the forty-year-old
suffrage amendment.

It passes by a margin of
one.

We burst into cheering
sing for victory
not tempering our mood
for more hurdles ahead.


## Tolerance

When I come home each day
wrapped in the worries and glow of suffrage
Arthur no longer
looks at me with disgust.

When I talk to Mother
about the latest suffrage news at dinner
Father doesn't excuse himself to the next room.

They have developed
a tolerance for me.
My conversations no longer provoke
red faces
anger
arguments.

It's one step forward.


## My New Job
February 1918

Our landlord sold Cameron House.
We have new headquarters
at Jackson Place—
across the park from Cameron House

still in view of
Lafayette
the White House
the Avenue.

Jackson Place keeps us close
to the president
close to the Capitol.

Mother helps us
move in
even attends NWP meetings.

NWP offers me a promotion—
switchboard operator
answering calls
with switches and wires
I know nothing about.

When I answer a call
for the first time
my hands shake
trying to remember how to connect
how to listen and write
all at the same time.

With the House pressing our amendment
I answer calls about the next steps.
Push the Senate to vote
yes.

It requires everyone's efforts.
And I have the power to push callers
to action.

# We Worry about Europe (and Sophie)

We get a letter from Sophie
in France.

I prayed the war would end
before her training ended stateside.

At least here
we knew she was safe.

Over there
I know she is needed.
But worry sits on my chest
weighs me down.


# I Answer a Few Hundred Questions by Telephone

Call 1:
*Hello?*
*National Woman's Party.*
*You've heard from the antis and not from us?*
*Well, we can remedy that.*
*Are you on our mailing list?*

Call 2:
*Hello?*
*National Woman's Party.*
*How do you join?*
*You can send in your dues*
*and we will send you copies*
*of the* Suffragist, *our newsletter,*
*so you can read what's really happening.*

Call 3:
*Hello?*
*National Woman's Party.*

*Can I deliver a message to the president?*
*You can call the White House switchboard.*
*He ignores our messages*
*but I'm sure he'd be delighted to hear from you.*

*Call 4:*
*Hello?*
*National Woman's Party.*
*Do I believe in suffrage?*
*Well, yes, I do.*
*I believe in it so much*
*I went to jail.*
*What's that?*
*Yes, my mother is proud of me.*

## Not Guilty of Any Offense
March 6, 1918

Not guilty.
Never should have arrested the pickets.
Picketing is not unlawful.

The judge in the District Court of Appeals
rules in favor of ten of our women
claims we did nothing wrong
claims jailing us was unconstitutional.

We'll see if the arresting officers
other judges
the wardens
take note in the future.

# War Comes to Washington
July 1918

With many men shipped off to Europe
people descend upon the city by train
even by foot
to help in the war effort.

Washington bulges with extra people
willing to help
needing shelter.

Mother and Father agree
to take in boarders
tuck away the extra cash
to help with the rising cost of food
that Father's stagnant pension
doesn't cover.

Newspaper reports deadly influenza rages
in Europe
in other parts of the United States.
With so many outsiders descending on Washington
will they bring it here
to my aging father?

Mother worries less about influenza
but insists anyone we squeeze into our home
must be for suffrage.

# Celebrating Inez
August 6, 1918

We throw a party to remember
Inez Milholland,
friend and suffrage martyr,
who died while on tour for suffrage.

It's odd to celebrate someone I've never met—
like lauding a dead president—
ignoring the faults
a symbol
not a person.

A hundred of us meet
at Lafayette's feet
with white, gold, purple banners
and banners with words:

WE PROTEST AGAINST
THE CONTINUED DISENFRANCHISEMENT
OF WOMEN FOR WHICH
THE PRESIDENT OF THE UNITED STATES
IS RESPONSIBLE.
WE DEMAND
THAT THE PRESIDENT AND HIS PARTY
SECURE THE PASSAGE
OF THE SUFFRAGE AMENDMENT
THROUGH THE SENATE
IN THE PRESENT SESSION.

Inez's own last words are with us:

HOW LONG MUST WOMEN WAIT
FOR LIBERTY?

But instead of our silence
we speak out.

Mrs. Lewis says,
*We are here because when our country*
*is at war for liberty and democracy . . .*
Before she can finish
police seize her
arrest her.

As soon as I see the handcuffs
hear the calloused voice
of the police
I shrink from the crowd
the clank of metal doors
slamming in my mind.

Hazel holds on to an American flag
speaks up.
*Here at the statue of Lafayette,*
*who fought for the liberty of this country,*
*and under the American flag,*
*I am asking for . . .*
They seize her
arrest her.
She never lets go of the American flag.

Police
arrest forty-eight of our women
for
*holding a meeting on public grounds*
or
*climbing a statue.*

I can't push
the memories
away.

So instead of reminding them
that protesting isn't unlawful
I retreat to the background
succumb to silence
again.

## Fear

each arrest
each boot stomp
each threat
brings me back to that night
to the fear
to the hunger pangs

it is a battle in my mind

to choose confidence
to choose persistence
to choose strength

instead of caving into
fear

## Press On

I'm at Jackson Place
setting up banners for another picket.

Our ladies
keep getting arrested

and released—
they don't know what to charge them with.

No judge wants to sentence them.
No warden wants to watch over them.

*You're here early,*
Lucy says.
She pours more coffee.

*I'm not going to let them scare me,*
I tell her.

Who?

*The police.*
*The crowds.*
*Myself.*

Lucy cracks a sly smile.
*It's okay to be scared.*
*Just don't let that stop you.*

We've lived through the worst.
I must press on.

## The Breaking Point
August 16, 1918

We could not stay away
from protesting at Lafayette Square
and Hazel was arrested again.
I never wanted Hazel to experience
what I did.

She told the judge,
*Women cannot be law-breakers,*
*until they are law-makers!*

But the judge didn't listen.
Police insist we need permits.
Our lawyers claim we are within the law.
She thought she'd be okay.
I thought she'd be okay—
stronger than me.

She came home from jail three days later
in an ambulance
weak from hunger-striking
sickened from dirty water.

Our minds might be made of steel
but our bodies aren't.

Her mother in Montana
would see the newspapers
so Hazel sent a telegram
to explain:
>               ITS SPLENDID
>               DONT WORRY

## Too Much Power
September 16, 1918

We set up another protest—
four o'clock
at Lafayette Monument.
President Wilson schedules
a meeting with us at two o'clock.

Wilson claims to be sympathetic
to our cause
even praises it.

Words of sympathy don't pass an amendment.

If he'd just speak up
speak out.
He needs to lobby
for us among senators.

His meeting
is an attempt to stop our protest
silence us
make us think things move forward
when they don't.

Some of our own ladies
are thrilled that the president pays us any mind.
They give too much power
to those in power.

## Wilson Relents
September 30, 1918

President Wilson pushes more
for our cause
speaking about it publicly
instead of behind closed doors.

*We have made partners of the women in this war;*
*shall we admit them only to a partnership*
*of suffering and sacrifice and toil*
*and not a partnership of privilege and right?*

President Wilson
pushes the Senate.

*The passage of this amendment
is a vitally necessary war measure.*

Finally, he speaks out
for women.

Finally, President Wilson
pushes our cause
one
step
forward.

Finally, some congressmen see
the work women do
for the war
and want to give us
a voice.

Behind closed doors
we celebrate this win.

## The Senate Has Its Turn
October 1, 1918

The Senate votes today
persuaded by Wilson's speech.
Rachel's boss,
Senator La Follette, is a yes
as are many of his colleagues
but we wait for confirmation.
The votes come in.

We hold our breath in the gallery
for each answer.

Defeat.

Suffrage is shy
two votes.

Two votes.
If only President Wilson
had pushed for suffrage soon—
pushed harder.
If only we had pushed harder.

The exhaustion worn on every suffragist's face—

we couldn't have done more.
We gave it everything.

Defeated.


## Spanish Influenza
October 1918

The paper announces the cause of death
in each obituary—
influenza
influenza
influenza.

Some of our ladies
have fallen ill
and I worry
they'll suffer the worst.

It spreads
everywhere—
on the war front
on the home front
to civilians and soldiers alike.

We stay home more.
Church is closed.

Each time I hear Father cough
it sends shivers up my spine.
Has it come to our house?

We follow all the precautions
listed in the papers:
>  Stay off streetcars.
>  Postpone unnecessary meetings.
>  Wear a gauze mask.

We don't want any of us
to become one of the numbers listed
but will it be enough?

All I can think about is
Sophie.
Is she sick over there?
We'd never find out in time
to pray for her.


## Mother Changes Her Focus

With schools shut down
churches closed
deaths on the rise
we have to be careful how much we protest
gather in groups.

Mother changes her focus.
The Red Cross needs her
more than suffrage.
She sews masks late into the night
at the kitchen table.
She makes one for me to wear
to work
hoping I won't get sick.
Mother does things that are needed
now
while I spend time
focused on the future.

I help with dinner
so she can keep sewing.
I chop onions
more than usual.
She tells me onions are known to prevent
influenza.
I worry the grocer is trying to swindle her.


## Hopeless

Am
I
the
only
one
who
feels
like
we
are
fighting
an
unwinnable

battle?
That
we
and
those
who
came
before
us
have
been
fighting
a
decades-long
fight
with
no
more
victory
today
than
then?
Am
I
the
only
one
discouraged
disenchanted
defeated?

# Change

I wake up
with a clearer view.
I will not dread the inevitability of jail—
they can't have that power anymore.
We will come out stronger.

With President Wilson finally on board
our pickets move from the White House
to the Capitol building.

Congress will see us
up close
with our banners

with our words.

Rachel warns me.
*It will be a different battle.*
*You must be diplomatic with the senators.*
*Many of them tried to pass the amendment.*

*We've been nothing but diplomatic,*
I tell her.

Her raised eyebrows question me.
*Congress won't see it that way.*

I leave for the Capitol
ready to do whatever it takes.

# Behind the Banners

Rose and I hold banners at the Capitol.
Police look away.
I break our silent oath
and ask Rose,
*Do you still have nightmares*
*from prison,*
*from hunger striking?*

*My darling,*
*I have nightmares*
*from the sanatorium.*
*But yes,*
*my body has never forgotten the way*
*hunger ate away at me in jail.*

*I still hear the boots,*
*the guards' sticks hitting the cells.*

*I still feel bugs crawling on me.*

Back and forth
we volley memories
get them out of our anxious minds
into the open.

*We wrote songs*
*in jail—*
*Alice and I.*
*Songs that poked fun at the guards.*
*We'd sing them*
*in whispers.*

*Did you ever get caught?*

*Only when we couldn't stop laughing*
*like two drunks.*
*They thought we were crazy—*
*especially Alice.*

As an anti-suffrage congressman
from Virginia
walks nearby
Rose starts singing:
*We asked him for the vote*
*as we stood,*
*as we stood.*
*We asked him for the vote*
*as we stood.*

# Words Afire
October 13, 1918

Sometimes standing isn't
enough.

Our group proceeds directly to the Senate floor—
the words of anti-suffrage senators
clutched in our hands
to be burned.

If the message of our protests
is not clear
on our banners
we will make ourselves clear
through our actions.

Capitol Police line up
ready to spar with us.
Senators step back.

We light a fire
in the Capitol.
Warmth invades
this coldhearted place—

I am arrested.

# They Do Nothing
When the judge lets me go
when there is no sentence
when I face no consequences for setting a fire in the Senate
even I am shocked.

I went to jail for much less.

# Some Consequences Are Worse than Jail

The judge did nothing to me
but Rachel comes home in a fury.

*How could you?*
she asks me.
*You knew that Senator La Follette*
*is for woman suffrage.*
*Yet you set fire to the place where I work?*
*The place where those laws are made?*

Mother and Father have strong opinions
but hold their tongues
and leave the room.

*Rachel,*
I begin.

*No.*
*You have no good excuse*
*other than you are radical.*
*I want suffrage just as much as you do*
*but you can't burn down the Capitol building*
*to get it.*

*I'm sorry, Rachel.*
*I—we didn't intend to hurt anyone.*

*You may not have burned anything down*
*but you lost the confidence*
*of some of your supporters.*

I wish I'd been sentenced to jail—
it would have been easier than this.

# Picket Day 657
October 28, 1918

Banners wave
in front of the Capitol
the next day.
Crowds gather
on their way to work.

Influenza spreading
worries everyone.
We mask up
hold banners outside.

WE DEMAND
AN AMENDMENT
TO THE
UNITED STATES
CONSTITUTION
ENFRANCHISING
WOMEN

The Capitol Police
see our Senate banners.

They arrest us
again.

Release us
again.

Arrest.

Release.

They put us in a basement
throwing one woman
injuring her
so that an ambulance
must come for her.

Our ladies
keep being harmed
at the hands
of small-minded men.

Jail did not break us.
We will not be broken.

## Meaningless Arrests

Are these arrests for show?
Attempts to scare us?
Keep us from protesting
again
and
again?

I don't know if
they'll change their minds—
take us back to the District Jail
railroad us back to the workhouse.

I don't know
what's for show
what's for real.
I shake uncontrollably
as the metal
cinches around
my wrists.

My mind is determined
but my body remembers
jail.

## Ceasefire
November 11, 1918

The Great War
is over in Europe.
Finally, something good
to read about in the paper
instead of the
number of deaths
from influenza.

I wait for news
about Sophie
while the president leaves for Paris
to negotiate the peace.

Wilson needs to bring peace
to the women of this country
who still need the democracy
he urged as a war measure.
Will he still support his
suffrage war measure
without his
war?

## Talk about Suffrage
I visit Rachel on Capitol Hill—
the guards stiffen when they see me.

*I'm here to visit my sister.*
*She works in Senator La Follette's office.*
They don't relax.

Rachel sits behind a small desk stacked high with papers.
*Matilda,*
*you're not here to—*
she darts her eyes around—
*burn something, are you?*

*Don't be silly,*
I say.
*But I am here to talk about suffrage.*
*What more can I do?*

*The senator is for suffrage.*
*No one to convince here.*
She leans in closer and whispers,
*But I can give you names*
*of senators*
*who are on the fence—*
*just no fires.*

## Urgency
November 19, 1918

We send out a flurry of letters
urging our women not to despair
as the Senate's session
comes to a close
and we lose our chance
for the amendment
this year.

Suffrage won't be a war measure
without a war.

We urge
      letter writing
      telegrams
      personal visits
in these last days.

Maybe
one of our members
can convince
her waffling senator to budge.

But we all know
senators will need more convincing
than just letters.

## Our Next Steps

I march with a group to the Senate
a fire burning within me.

ALL AMERICAN WOMEN PROTEST
AGAINST THE SENATE'S RECESSING
WITHOUT PASSING
THE SUFFRAGE AMENDMENT

Every step I take,
I tell myself:
Persist.
Persist.
Persist.

# How Close Is Close?

It is late when I drag myself home
each evening
feet blistered, sore.

Mother sets dinner in front of me—
it was hot three hours ago.

I don't mind the cold food
as long as it fills my stomach.
Most days I don't take time
to eat.

*Matilda,*
*you must take care of yourself.*
*You'll fall ill.*

I nod
trying to keep my eyes open long enough
to finish eating.

*Can you stay home for a few days?*
*The influenza seems to be all over the city.*

*I can't stop now.*
*We are so close.*

*Are we really?*
*We've been close for years.*
Mother's voice is tired—
too tired to allow herself to be hopeful again.

I wash my dish
head upstairs
too tired to argue.

I don't know how close we are.
I have lost all perspective.

Everything caves in on me—
war's end
influenza's rampage
my utter exhaustion.

## Time Off

I take a few days off for the holidays
to sleep.

Mother tries to fatten me up.
I want to tell her and Father
I'm saving money
for my own apartment.

But I might waste away
without Mother's food.

## Another Pinning

December 15, 1918

Hazel gets her pin
a badge of honor
for jail time
on behalf of suffrage.

I clap for her
and the other women
getting pinned.

I wonder how long
the nightmares of jail

will stay
with all of us.

Forever
I suspect.


## Picket Day 722
January 1, 1919

I enter the new year
rested
and angry.

The first day of the new year
starts with flames outside the White House.

We set up urns
at the White House gates
protest the president again
for his lack of action
on behalf of the women
in his own country.
Mrs. Lewis begins,
*President Wilson is deceiving the world*
*when he appears as the prophet of democracy . . .*
She throws his speech
into the flames.

Soldiers and sailors watch.
I can't stop the way my heart races
my breathing falters.

They attack
overturn the urn
stomp out the flames.

Another group begins a new fire
in Lafayette Park.

There are fires
everywhere.

## Do You Still Get Scared?

Lucy moves slower than usual.
Miss Paul too.
The injuries from jail
weigh on them
alongside the
wait for the vote.

They sit quietly at the table
reading through newspapers.
I gather copies of President Wilson's speeches
to make a good fire.

Lucy puts her hand on mine
to still me.
*Don't think we haven't noticed
the change in you.
You're braver.*

I never feel brave
but I'm brave enough to ask:
*Do you ever still feel scared
about going to jail?*
I ask them,
*Do you ever have
nightmares?*

I still feel
the twinge of hunger pangs.

I still jump
when I hear the click of shoes on concrete.
I still shake
when I see the police.

They both stare at me.
Of course they're not scared.

*All the time,*
Miss Paul says.

*The nightmares never go away.*
Lucy sighs.

*Jail is necessary*
*but not a joy.*

I toss the president's speeches in a basket
with wood.

*You know what to do,*
Lucy tells me.
*You lead.*
*Others follow.*


## How to Be Your Own Girl

Forge your own path.
Pursue your own passions.
Know who you are.
Don't let anyone put out your fire.

## Picket Day 724
### January 3, 1919

We see how high the flames can go
brushing the tips of the tree leaves.
I throw page after page
into flames.

Until one policeman
wrestles them out of my hands
papers fly all over the sidewalk
full of wind
as the words themselves.

They clamp their handcuffs
around my wrists.

## They Fall Away

Some NWP members
don't approve
of lighting up the president's words.

Some NWP members
wish us to calm down now.

Some NWP members
sit in the comfort of their homes
writing letters about how we should act.

Every step we've taken
someone thinks it's too much.

They can fight
in their own way.

# Picket Day 728
### January 7, 1919

The president is in Europe
talking peace in Italy.

Hazel and I begin another flame
at the White House
in an iron urn.
I wonder when
I can burn my mask
along with Wilson's words?

I take the words
of the president's latest speech
and read them aloud.
I stammer at first
then speak clearly:

*Being free.*
*America desires to show others*
*how they may also share*
*in the freedom of the world.*

I toss them into the flame.
They turn to ash.

I am arrested
for proving the president's words
mean nothing.

## Closing In

The tightening of the handcuffs
the smallness of the Black Maria
the closeness of the police
makes me

*gasp*
*gasp*
*gasp*

*g    a    s    p.*

Even in my determination
no matter how many arrests
I am crushed
every time.

Lingering smoke
taints my clothes.
The sting of Wilson's words remains.
I yearn for freedom—
the hum of the city
the blue of the sky
the walks where my feet take me anywhere
I choose to go.

## Sophie's Return

They let me go again
but one day, I worry
my luck will run out
again.

We hadn't heard from Sophie
in weeks
but when her face pops up
at the kitchen door
we all think Mother
has seen a mouse.
The squeals
soon turn to happy tears
a huddle of hugs.

Sophie's bright spirit
is home
but there's a darkness on her face—
the deaths she's seen
haunt her.

We tread lightly
but she hugs freely
like always.

*You did it,*
she whispers.

I nod
knowing that in our time apart
we've experienced things
we speak about only in whispers.

# Walking with Sophie

I usually walk alone
but Sophie walks with me
arm-in-arm. We-walk-in-silence—
worry written on Sophie's face.
Both of our hearts sting—
the torture in jail still taunts me,
the images that must haunt Sophie.
Even though I have a sense
of urgency in my work
in the quiet I am not fully
healed. I suspect Sophie
isn't either. Maybe walking
will help us mend. Maybe
the strength I've discovered
within will help Sophie find
her footing again.

# The Nights Come

When the darkness comes
I hear Sophie
tossing
sniffling
in bed.

I move closer.
Her whole body shakes.

I wrap my arms around her
until she falls asleep.

Just like Rachel did for me.

# Picket Day 732
### January 11, 1919

I am arrested
again—
for fires
in front of the White House.

I brace myself.
I know what awaits
this time.

I thought I could
never endure jail
again.
But I can endure—
that much I have learned.

## No Mercy

When the judge hands us the first sentence
of the new year—
five days—
I applaud.

He seems shocked by the once-silent suffragist
who mocks him.

I get three more days
for that spectacle.

I can survive eight days.

They cart me to
District Jail.

## It's Different This Time

No one tries to harm us
or mock us this time.
They even give us blankets.
I count down the days
until I am free.

Cold cell walls
and gigantic rats
are part of the job.

I will not eat.
The hunger strike
weakens my body
but strengthens my spirit.

But at night
the clomp of the guards' boots
still throw me back two years.

I've changed since then
but my body remembers.

## Breakdown

When I get home
I'm dirty
cold to the core.

Sophie puts her arms around me
draws a warm bath.
Mother makes broth.

Jail takes a toll.
My body
betrays me.

# Picket Day 763
February 11, 1919

We carry the picture
of President Wilson
on a stretcher
from Jackson Place
to the White House gates.
We cart urns
wood
banners
speeches
in a long line.
We burn the speeches
and the president
in effigy.

Thousands watch.

It takes a hundred policemen
to gather and cart off
thirty-six of us.

## Too Far
No jail this time.
They make us wait
in the police precinct
offer us sandwiches.
     (Sandwiches!)

Have they finally realized
wormy meals and torture
only strengthen our resolve?
Are they trying to be friendly?
     (Have they poisoned the sandwiches?)

Many women in the NWP
have abandoned us
say we have gone too far.
Even my mother can't believe
I'm still at it
that I am disrespecting
the president's words.

We have not gone far
enough
if we still do not have suffrage.

## We Are Close

These days
tick by.
A sense of urgency
propels each of us.

We are too close
to grow weary.

We grip the dream of the vote
so tightly
we might suffocate one another.

We work late
writing letters
drafting speeches.

I spend many nights
at Jackson Place
collapsing into an extra bed
meant for out-of-towners.

I lie awake—
no longer afraid—
reeling with ideas
of how we can push
one more congressman
one more senator
one more man
who needs to know.
His voice
coupled with ours
can change
everything.

## Reunion

One morning after I didn't come home
Sophie brings biscuits to headquarters—
Mother insisted.

Joy walks in—
a surprise to all.
We reunite
in a heap of hugs.

Our lives
changed and scarred
since the last time we were together
in one room.

Joy's bags are packed
for a long suffrage trip
but she eats Mother's biscuits
with us
like we did
before marriage and wars and jail.

# Prison Special
February 15, 1919

Twenty-six of our ladies
tour by train
through the country
tell about imprisoned suffragists.
They wear prison outfits—
by choice this time.
I stay in Washington
not wanting to
relive
what I went through.

The ladies talk to women in
Charleston
Jacksonville
Chattanooga
New Orleans
San Antonio
Los Angeles
San Francisco
Denver
Chicago
Milwaukee
Detroit
Syracuse
Boston
Hartford
New York.

We will need their voices
when it's their state's turn
to ratify our amendment.

Telling ordinary people what has happened
in Washington
to our women
in jail.

*How did we not know?*
they say.

We must keep telling our story
until everyone has heard.


## Optimism

The switchboard at NWP headquarters
never stops ringing
and I am there
answering every call.

There's a fervor
in the air
that cannot be quashed.

Optimism
runs through our ladies
that I haven't seen in years.

We think . . .
We believe . . .
We hope . . .

Each sentence begins
with a dream.

Each rumor of passage
makes us pray
for a miracle.

## Yes #1
May 21, 1919

The House of Representatives
rallies again—
enough of them say
YES!


## Back to the Senate
With one yes
we must push.
We call.
We visit senators.
We keep track of their votes
on a board at headquarters.

The Hill is a flurry
of chatter
telegrams
insistence.
We need their yeses too.


## Sleepless Nights
Rachel comes home at night
hopeful.

The Senate is going to go for suffrage.
She is sure.

I am not.

But it's hard to dismiss her squeals.
Neither one of us sleeps.

## Yes #2
June 4, 1919

The Senate stalls
no longer.
They eke out support
for our amendment.

YES!

## Cause for Celebration
We celebrate at dinner—
Mother
Rachel
Sophie
me.
We miss Joy.

Mother announces,
*I've changed my membership*
*to the NWP.*
We can't hide
our surprise
our relief.
*I don't always approve of the tactics,*
*but there's work still to be done.*
*And I think we should do it together.*

She squeezes my hand.

Father joins in on the celebration
with a box of Hershey's Kisses.

Even Arthur eats one.

# To the States
June 1919

1.
Ratification of this amendment
we've worked hard for
will have to be earned
state by state
until we get enough.

2.
We need three-fourths of the state governments to vote
YES.
There are forty-eight states.

3.
Only thirty-six states
to say
YES.

# Thirty-Five Yeses
June 1919–July 1920

For a full year
we petition
each state—
send letters
delegations
beg them to lobby
state lawmakers.

For a year
I'm tied to the phone
at the NWP headquarters.

Talking to women
across the country.
Writing letters.
I sleep here
too tired to go home.

Hope rises
with each yes.
Hope dashes
with states that refuse.

Finally, thirty-five states
are won over.

With each state
Miss Paul stitches
a star on the banner.

## The Last Star
August 18, 1920

Tennessee comes in last—
the vote that clinched the amendment—
thanks to one man who voted
because his mother urged him to.

Alice Paul sews the final star
hangs the ratification flag
from the outside balcony

seen from the White House gates
where we stood
for so long
waiting for this day.

# It Is Law
August 26, 1920

This morning
under the cloak of darkness
Secretary of State Colby signed
the Nineteenth Amendment
into law.

No suffragists were invited.
Not NAWSA.
Not NWP.
Not one woman who fought for the amendment
was invited.
They wanted to avoid a spectacle
a celebration
an acknowledgment of all our work.

Anger and anguish
indignation and victory
suffering and suffrage
mark the journey.

We
will
celebrate
our amendment
and the women who pushed it
forward.

# I Allow Myself to Cry
I knew that women in Washington
wouldn't get to vote—
Arthur and Father and every man in the city
face the same barrier.

After all the angry mail
all the phone calls
all the cold days standing
all the arrests
all the jail time
all the hunger striking.

I want to celebrate this win.

But first
I sit in the lavatory
and let the tears out.

## Suffrage Won

Any suffragists in town gather at Jackson Place
and walk to Poli Theater.

Secretary of State Colby speaks on behalf of President Wilson:

> *Nothing has given me more pleasure*
> *than to do what I could to hasten the day*
> *when the womanhood of America*
> *could be recognized on the equal footing it deserves.*

Suffragists from the other organizations applaud
but our NWPs just sit stunned.
Wilson barely moved a finger
didn't pay us any mind when we were standing
in front of his house.

Miss Paul isn't invited to speak
still snubbed by the more proper Wilson-coddling suffragists.

Regardless of how any one of us feel about each other
the Nineteenth Amendment is official.

## My Own Place

I rent a room of my own
with my own money.
Arthur carries up a hand-me-down set of drawers
where I put feathers
scores of buttons
my suffrage collection
my sachet of notes from Sophie.

Rachel hands me a box.
*From Father,*
she says.
He's unable to make the trip
up the narrow stairway to my new room.

I unwrap the brown paper.
*My own box of Hershey Kisses.*

*Joy would be so excited to see this,*
Sophie says.
*You in your own place,*
*by yourself.*

Mother empties my suitcase quietly.
She gives me a hug
and a bag of sandwiches.

*Don't forget to eat,*
she reminds me.

They leave me
in the room alone—
so different than the last room
where I was on my own.
This one is cozy
and safe.

# At Least Someone Gets to Vote
October 29, 1920

Alice Paul doesn't travel home
to New Jersey
to vote.

She gathers us all to Jackson Place.

We watch
as Miss Paul fills out her ballot
voting for president of the United States for the first time.

She hands it off
to Catherine Flanagan to notarize
appointed for this task by the president himself.

She drops it in the mail
and we all
dissolve
into cheers
and tears.

# Election Day Walk
### November 2, 1920

Today
instead
of
walking
to
the
polls
I
saunter
to
Jackson
Place.
I'm
not
the
fourteen-
year-
old
that
snuck
out
to
watch
the
procession.
Yet
still
her.
Changed.
Ready
to
make
more

change.
There
is
still
work
to
do.


## What's Next?
Days after our country elects Warren G. Harding
as the next president
Jackson Place slowly comes back to life.

Though many got what they wanted
they voted
and didn't return.

Miss Paul has much more on her mind—
a suffragist sculpture for the Capitol building
to honor Susan B. Anthony
Lucretia Mott
Elizabeth Cady Stanton—
women who came before us.
We need to raise money for the statue.
Miss Paul wants to hold
the NWP convention here
in February.
Much planning must be done.
But more than anything
Miss Paul wants to fight
for an Equal Rights Amendment.

Lucy packs up her things.
The silence between her and Miss Paul
makes me leave the room—

I have phone calls to make.
Lucy is ready for fewer battles.
She's done and heading home for good.

I stay, for now.
The work continues.
It may always continue.
Even if we leave this building
even if I take another job
I doubt fighting for our rights will ever be
completely done
in my lifetime.

Maybe a hundred years from now
other nineteen-year-olds
won't have to be jailed
for their rights.

# Afterword

The earliest Matilda would have been able to vote in Washington, DC, was November 3, 1964—forty-four years after white women got the vote.

Washington, DC, residents couldn't vote for president until 1964. They couldn't vote for local officials until 1973.

We don't have evidence of Matilda voting in 1964, but as hard as she fought for suffrage, it's hard to imagine that she would have missed it.

**"Women have suffered agony of soul which you can never comprehend, that you and your daughters might inherit political freedom. That vote has been costly. Prize it!"**

**—CARRIE CHAPMAN CATT, 1920**

# Dramatis Personae

Nearly every character in the book, with only a couple of exceptions, was a real person. I dug up what I could find that was true about each person. As much as I could ascertain from the historical record, I put them in real places and real events. But where the research was silent, I utilized artistic license to explore the feelings and conflicts they might have experienced.

The people listed here were real people. Matilda's neighbor, Peter, was someone I created for the story. I also had to cut two of Matilda's real sisters for the sake of story—Louise Bayard Young, her older sister, and Mary Ryan Young, her younger sister.

**MATILDA YOUNG**—Matilda was known as the youngest suffragist and the youngest to be jailed for her actions. I took on the voice of Matilda through the first-person point of view and used artistic license for her thoughts. I imagined that she would have gained confidence as the years went on.

After the amendment passed, Matilda and her mother attended the NWP Convention in 1921 as the delegates from Washington, DC. In the late 1920s to the early 1930s, Matilda and her younger sister, Mary, went to Europe with suffrage benefactor Alva Belmont. In the 1940s, she once again lived in Washington, DC, where she founded and directed the Children's Museum of Washington, DC. In 1945, she became a founding member of the Children's Book Guild, an organization with authors, illustrators, editors, and librarians that still exists.

It doesn't appear that Matilda ever married. She died in 1988 and is buried in Maryland.

**MOTHER (HARRIET ODEN YOUNG)**—Hattie was a suffragist and twenty years younger than her husband. In the book I make her a fan of the more conservative NAWSA and resistant to the militant tactics of the NWP. We don't know of her thoughts at the time. However, she did serve as a delegate to the NWP Convention in 1921. We do know that she was a suffragist and that she went to Occoquan to check on Matilda. She didn't work outside the house for many decades, but the 1930 census shows that she was working at a hospital.

**FATHER (LUDWIG YOUNG)**—He worked for the Census Bureau, and the family lived on Eighteenth Street in Northwest Washington, DC. We know from the historical record that many women had husbands who disapproved of their wives' and daughters' participation. I chose to make Matilda's father anti-suffrage to start with to illustrate the possible tensions between family members.

**JOY YOUNG ROGERS**—Joy was an active suffragist. She spent a lot of time traveling for the NWP, educating women across the country, giving speeches, and signing women up to join NWP. She worked on an antiwar journal with Merrill Rogers, whom she married.

**ARTHUR YOUNG**—Arthur was a shipping clerk for a department store in Washington, DC. I imagined that being the only boy in a large house of girls, there might have been arguments and disagreements.

**SOPHIA SINCLAIR YOUNG STOKES**—Sophia, known as Sophie, was Matilda's big sister and served in the Army Corps of Nurses in World War I. She married and became Sophie Stokes.

**RACHEL WILSON YOUNG LA FOLLETTE**—Rachel married Bob La Follette Jr., a senator from Wisconsin. She met him when she served as the secretary for his father (Senator Robert La Follette Sr.) on Capitol Hill.

**ALICE PAUL**—Alice's name is well-known as one of the militant suffragists—the ringleader. She spent a lot of time in the District Jail but never went to Occoquan Workhouse. After the Nineteenth Amendment was passed, she went back to school to earn three law degrees—a bachelor's, master's, and doctorate, all from American

University Washington College of Law. She wanted to better understand how laws were written. She also worked tirelessly on the Equal Rights Amendment, which has yet to pass as of 2024. Alice died in 1977 and devoted her whole life to equal rights for women.

**LUCY BURNS**—After women got the vote, Lucy chose not to work for the Equal Rights Amendment like her fellow suffrage leader, Alice Paul. Instead, she returned home to Brooklyn, New York. Her younger sister died in childbirth, and she raised her infant niece. She also devoted herself to the Catholic Church and volunteered for them. She died in 1966 at the age of eighty-seven.

We don't know if Lucy ever knew Matilda well, but we do know that they were in jail together at Occoquan on the Night of Terror.

**ROSE WINSLOW**—Her passport application from 1921 lists her as Ruza Wenclawska or Ruza Lyons (she was married to Phil Lyons). After the Nineteenth Amendment was passed, Rose Winslow performed on Broadway as Ruza Wenclawska. She was also a writer. She died in 1977 at the age of eighty-eight.

Rose and Matilda protested and were arrested together. It seemed probable that they would have known each other.

**HAZEL HUNKINS**—Hazel received a degree in chemistry from Vassar but had difficulty finding work as a chemist because she was a woman. She traveled for the NWP, stood at the White House gates as a Silent Sentinel, and was arrested several times. She married in 1920 and moved to London. Over her long life, she worked as a foreign correspondent for the *Chicago Tribune*, was an economic analyst, and continued to work for equal rights for women.

Hazel was just a few years older than Matilda Young, and though I don't know if they knew each other for certain, they did volunteer and get arrested during the same time, so it's likely they knew each other.

## Author's Note

Occoquan Workhouse is close to my home. When I first moved to the Virginia suburbs of Washington, DC, we explored the prison that has now been turned into an arts center. There is a museum in one of the buildings for the suffragists imprisoned there. While I had heard of Susan B. Anthony and Elizabeth Cady Stanton growing up, I had not heard of Lucy Burns or any of the other women imprisoned at Occoquan, and I didn't know they were tortured and force-fed. After a few visits to the museum, I knew I had to write about the women who many people might not know about. I didn't know that Matilda Young, jailed at nineteen, was part of the cause, and I imagined what it must have been like to be a young adult activist at a time when women were expected to follow traditional roles. These young women decided to reject those expectations and speak out against the things they didn't agree with—even when there were severe consequences.

The suffragists imprisoned at the Occoquan Workhouse were part of the National Woman's Party (NWP), which had split with the more moderate National American Woman Suffrage Association (NAWSA). The NWP was pretty radical for the time. No one had ever staged a demonstration in front of the White House. And to do it at a time of war was even more brazen.

There were hundreds of women who spent time as pickets in the front of the White House. Some devoted their lives to it—like Lucy Burns and Alice Paul. Others did it intermittently, coming in for a special day here or there.

I chose to give voice to Matilda Young because she was the youngest suffragist jailed. Out of all the women I researched, she's also not very famous. Yet, in my mind, what she did was extraordinary.

I combed through books, the National Woman's Party records, historical photos, and copies of the *Suffragist* newsletter, trying to find details. I dove into Matilda's Central High School yearbooks and visited museums. I walked from her street to her high school and imagined what her day-to-day life would have been. My goal was to allow the reader to feel what it felt like to be a teen in those moments in history. I used what was available, and by the power of historical fiction, I allowed my imagination to fill in the details when I couldn't find historical reference.

# Fact vs. Fiction

There is no evidence I found that Matilda Young was at the 1913 Woman Suffrage Procession, but I like to believe that she knew about it and that she supported it. Since Matilda lived in the city, she would have at least seen or heard about it. Her sister Joy Young was very involved in the NWP. Their mother was also a suffragist, though I didn't find any records that Harriet Oden Young picketed or went to jail for suffrage. It seemed probable that the talk of suffrage would have been prevalent in Matilda's life.

We know she began working at the NWP headquarters as a switchboard operator in 1918.

In the 1940s, Matilda founded a children's museum in Washington, DC. She had odd collections of dolls, minerals, and taxidermied animals in her museum. It seemed only fitting that she might have started collecting in her earlier life.

We don't know the first day Matilda decided to picket—only the days of her arrests. Many protested and weren't arrested, so it's probable that she could've been picketing for a few weeks or a few months before being arrested.

We know that the Silent Sentinel banners were made off-site. One park ranger told me that someone would go to the shop where the banners were being made to figure out what the messages from the NWP would be for the next day. It's an interesting story, and I decided that Matilda would be a good choice to pick them up.

What I know about Matilda's siblings and parents I learned from census data, a few newspaper articles, Find a Grave website, a few articles, and letters Matilda wrote from Europe after the vote was won. I have no idea if her father or her brother, Arthur, disapproved of her suffrage work. However, most men at that time weren't allies of suffrage—at least in the beginning.

It is likely that Matilda didn't vote for president until 1964 because residents of Washington, DC, truly could not vote for president until the Twenty-Third Amendment was passed in 1961. They couldn't vote for their city officials until 1973. Even today, DC residents do not have a voting member of Congress. Based on the records I've found, Matilda lived and worked in Washington, DC, her whole life, except for a few years in Europe. I imagine it would have been difficult to help win the vote and then not get it yourself for forty-four more years.

# African American Women Suffragists

As progressive as the NWP and NAWSA were for their time, they weren't very progressive when it came to including African American suffragists. In 1896, the National Association of Colored Women was formed, and Mary Church Terrell, an African American activist, served as president. She spoke at NAWSA conventions and was a member of several suffrage organizations—both Black and white. However, in most cases, Black women were discouraged from joining white woman suffrage organizations and then faced discrimination even if they were members.

During the March 1913 Woman Suffrage Procession, Ida B. Wells-Barnett, a journalist and organizer of the Alpha Suffrage Club, wanted to walk with the other women from Illinois. The Congressional Union, run by Alice Paul and Lucy Burns, encouraged the women to stay in their spot in the back of the march. Ida worked her way up to the Illinois delegation and walked with them anyway.

Even though Alice Paul was a Quaker and believed in the equality of all people, she knew that the women in her organization would disagree with her. The white Southern suffragists held a lot of power and forced Alice Paul to segregate the procession or they wouldn't participate at all. Ida Wells-Barnett was not the only Black woman to join the white marchers from her state. Black women from Delaware, New York, West Virginia, and Michigan also marched with their fellow white suffragists. Women from Howard University, a historically Black college in Washington, DC, walked with other college students.

Mary Church Terrell was invited by Alice Paul to come protest with her daughter. She talks about this in her autobiography, *A Colored Woman in a White World*. She says she did protest on several occasions but skipped one time she was asked. On that day, women were arrested and taken to Occoquan. I chose to have Matilda reflect on Mrs. Terrell's involvement, though I don't know if they ever met on those days.

Once the Nineteenth Amendment was ratified in 1920, African

American women and men continued to be discriminated against through poll taxes, literacy tests, and outright denial of voting, and they had to push for the Voting Rights Act of 1965 to use the voting power granted to them in previous constitutional amendments. Even today, more than a hundred years after the amendment was passed, many people from marginalized backgrounds still face obstacles when going to the polls. For more information about voter suppression, I suggest the books *One Person, No Vote* by Carol Anderson and *Democracy in One Book or Less* by David Litt.

As much as I wanted Lucy and Alice to stand up for disenfranchised Black women, I discovered a sobering truth—our heroes are flawed humans. We look back on history and wish they would have done more, but I didn't want to write revisionist history.

Because Matilda was only fourteen, and not involved in the movement at that time, it's unlikely she would have known the details of the disagreement between Alice Paul and the African American suffragists at the 1913 parade.

It is my hope that readers will seek out books that tell of the activism of the Black suffragists. They ran into many more obstacles than upper-class white women. For a thorough history of African American women suffragists, I recommend *African American Women in the Struggle for the Vote 1850–1920* by Rosalyn Terborg-Penn. Several of the books in the "For Further Reading" section include more about the African American women prominent in the suffrage movement.

As of the writing of this book, the editors of the Women in Suffrage Movements database are attempting to collect biographies of as many suffragists as possible. The links to some of the African American suffragists can be found here: https://documents.alexanderstreet .com/c/1007600702.

# Voting in 1920

Even though white women technically gained the vote in 1920, voter turnout among them was low. Only about 36 percent of eligible women voted in the 1920 election. In Virginia, where discriminatory practices for Black voters were rampant, only 6 percent of women voted in 1920. Some states required voter registration six months prior to an election. By the time the Nineteenth Amendment was passed in August 1920, the deadline for voter registration had already passed.

Once the Nineteenth Amendment was passed, NAWSA dissolved their organization and created the League of Women Voters (which still exists today) to engage in "get out the vote" campaigns. They also hosted citizenship schools.

## Your Turn

Throughout the entire research, writing, and revising process for this book, I never ceased to be amazed at the great sacrifice that suffragists made for our right to vote. Some of them gave up considerable time, money, and comfort. Inez Milholland died pursuing suffrage for women. Others nearly died from the abuse and hunger strikes in prison.

Our democracy works best when citizens are involved—when we stay informed about current events and policies, when we vote, and when we let our elected leaders know how we feel about issues.

You can make a difference. Get involved with the issues that you care about. Write to your congressional leaders. Write to your local and state representatives. Volunteer for causes that matter to you.

Maybe you're not old enough to vote yet. Matilda wasn't old enough to vote when she got involved with suffrage. None of the women she worked with were allowed to vote. Yet they persisted. You can too.

# Timeline

| | |
|---|---|
| May 4, 1912 | Mabel Ping-Hua Lee leads a suffrage parade in NYC at age sixteen. |
| March 3, 1913 | Woman Suffrage Procession, Washington, DC |
| March 4, 1913 | Woodrow Wilson is inaugurated as president for his first term. |
| November 21, 1913 | Lucy Burns is arrested for chalking the sidewalk. |
| February 1914 | Congressional Union and NAWSA go their separate ways. |
| February 14, 1916 | Suffragists make valentines for congressmen. |
| June 1916 | Matilda Young graduates from Central High School. |
| November 7, 1916 | Woodrow Wilson is reelected. |
| November 25, 1916 | Inez Milholland dies after collapsing at a suffrage event. |
| January 9, 1917 | Suffragists visit President Wilson to honor Inez Milholland and to address suffrage. |
| January 10, 1917 | First day of Silent Sentinel protests |
| February 18, 1917 | Working Women protest |
| March 4–5, 1917 | President Wilson's second inauguration (private ceremony and swearing in on March 4 and public event on March 5) |
| April 6, 1917 | The United States enters the Great War (World War I). |
| June 20, 1917 | Silent Sentinels hold the Russian banner. |
| June 22, 1917 | Women are arrested for the first time at the White House gates. |

| | |
|---|---|
| June 26, 1917 | More women are arrested, and they become the first to go to jail. |
| July 14, 1917 | Bastille Day protests |
| July 19, 1917 | Women in jail are pardoned by the president. |
| August 6, 1917 | Many arrests are made. |
| August 14, 1917 | Silent Sentinels hold the Kaiser Wilson banner. |
| September 4, 1917 | Parade of drafted men with Woodrow Wilson |
| September 7, 1917 | Dudley Field Malone resigns his post with the Wilson administration and becomes much more involved in representing the suffragists. |
| October 6, 1917 | Matilda Young is arrested for the first time. |
| October 20, 1917 | Seven women are arrested, including Alice Paul and Rose Winslow. |
| November 12, 1917 | Matilda is arrested along with other women and sentenced to time in Occoquan Workhouse. |
| November 14–15, 1917 | Night of Terror in Occoquan Workhouse |
| November 23, 1917 | Women at Occoquan go to court and are moved to the District Jail. |
| November 27–28, 1917 | Women, including Matilda Young, are released from prison. |
| December 6, 1917 | Matilda and other women who were jailed receive a pin to honor their time in jail. |
| January 10, 1918 | House of Representatives votes for the suffrage amendment, and it passes by a margin of one. |
| February 1918 | National Woman's Party headquarters moves from Cameron House to Jackson Place, still at Lafayette Square. |

| | |
|---|---|
| August 6, 1918 | Women are arrested at a protest that honored Inez Milholland. |
| September 30, 1918 | President Wilson encourages Senate to pass the suffrage amendment as a war measure. |
| October 1, 1918 | Senate votes on the suffrage amendment; it fails by two votes. |
| October 13, 1918 | Matilda Young is arrested at the Capitol building. |
| October 25, 1918 | Matilda Young is arrested. |
| October 28, 1918 | Matilda Young is arrested. |
| November 11, 1918 | The Great War ends. |
| January 1, 1919 | Watchfires begin at the White House. |
| January 3, 1919 | Matilda Young is arrested at a watchfire. |
| January 7, 1919 | Matilda Young is arrested for setting President Wilson's words on fire. |
| January 11, 1919 | Matilda Young goes to the District Jail. |
| February 15, 1919 | Women leave for Prison Special by train across the country, telling about their time in jail. |
| May 21, 1919 | House of Representatives votes to pass the suffrage amendment. |
| June 4, 1919 | Senate votes to pass the suffrage amendment. |
| June 1919–August 1920 | States legislatures meet to vote on the amendment. |
| August 18, 1920 | Tennessee becomes the thirty-sixth (and last) state needed to pass the amendment. |
| August 26, 1920 | Nineteenth Amendment officially becomes law. |
| November 2, 1920 | First election day after Nineteenth Amendment is passed |
| June 2, 1924 | Snyder Act is passed, granting people of Native Nations the benefits of citizenship, including voting (though in |

|                    | practice many didn't get the right to vote until decades later). |
|--------------------|------------------------------------------------------------------|
| March 29, 1961     | Twenty-Third Amendment is passed, allowing DC residents to vote for president and vice president. |
| November 3, 1964   | First presidential election that DC residents vote for president |
| August 6, 1965     | The Voting Rights Act prohibits discrimination in voting (no more poll taxes or literacy tests) and also provides language assistance, including translated ballots. |

# Quotes

I have used italics to denote dialogue through the poems. Some of the dialogue is documented. Some I made up. The dialogue that is documented in research is indicated in this section. The banner wordings in all caps in the poems are quoted as found in photos, actual banners on view at museums, and in articles I read from the time period.

Page 13: *Men for Women*—"Henpecko . . . Where are your skirts?"
US Senate Committee on the District of Columbia. "Report of the Committee on the District of Columbia with Hearings and List of Witnesses, 63rd Congress." In *Women's Suffrage and the Police: Three Senate Documents*. New York: Arno Press & *New York Times*, 1971.

Page 27: *One Sentence*—"The rights of citizens of the United States . . ."
Joint Resolution of Congress Proposing a Constitutional Amendment Extending the Right of Suffrage to Women, May 19, 1919. Ratified Amendments, 1795–1992; General Records of the United States Government; Record Group 11; National Archives. www.archives.gov/historical-docs/19th-amendment.

Page 32: *Losing Allies*—"You may think we are all a set of old fogies . . ."
Letter from Anna Howard Shaw (NAWSA leader) to Lucy Burns. Zahniser, J. D., and Amelia R. Fry. *Alice Paul: Claiming Power*. New York: Oxford University Press, 2014.

Pages 35–36: *Valentines*—all valentines
"Valentines for Congressmen in the Mails Today." *Fall River Daily Globe*, February 14, 1916.

Page 39: *Four More Years of Wilson*—"I wish you had the vote."
"Mr. Wilson, How Do You Feel about Woman Suffrage Now?" *Suffragist* 4, no. 46 (November 1916): 10.

Page 56: *The Press*—"Their purpose is to make it impossible . . ."
"'Picket' the White House." *Washington Post*, January 10, 1917.

Page 56: *Private Letters*—"I wish to make a protest . . ."

Letter from Tacie Paul to Alice Paul. Walton, Mary. *A Woman's Crusade: Alice Paul and the Battle for the Ballot.* New York: St Martin's Griffin, 2015.

Page 62: *Stories from the Line*—"I brought my little boy down especially to see you girls . . ."

Letter from Hazel Hunkins to her mother. Papers of Hazel Hunkins-Hallinan, 1864–1984. Radcliffe Institute, https://mhs .mt.gov/education/Women/HHLessonPlanFinal2.pdf.

Page 76: *Another Miracle*—"In the past there have been no pickets . . ."

"Women 'Wage Earners' First Sunday 'Silent Picket' at the White House." *Washington Post*, February 19, 1917.

Page 84: *The Great War*—"We shall fight . . ."

President Wilson's Declaration of War Message to Congress, April 2, 1917. Records of the United States Senate; Record Group 46; National Archives. www.archives.gov/milestone-documents /address-to-congress-declaration-of-war-against-germany? _ga=2.2332280.915573898.1709834833-557581696.1708710914.

Page 92: *Deepest Cuts*—"Unwise, unpatriotic . . ."

"Crowds Again Rend Suffrage Banners." *New York Times*, June 22, 1917.

Page 93: *Bedtime Reading*—"Bad Manners, Mad Banners"

"'Bad Manners, Mad Banners' of the White House Pickets." *Washington Post*, April 23, 1917.

Page 97: *Two Kinds of Men*—"Girls, you are right . . ."

Evans, Ernestine. "An Hour on the Suffrage Picket Line." *Suffragist* 5, no. 64 (1917): 5.

Page 106: *Picket Day 163*—conversation between the police chief and Alice Paul

Stevens, Doris. *Jailed for Freedom: American Women Win the Vote.* Edited by Carol O'Hare. Troutdale, OR: NewSage Press, 1995, 75. Edited from original edition first published in 1920.

Page 112: *Picket Day 168*—"Unpatriotic . . ."

Stevens, Doris. *Jailed for Freedom: American Women Win the Vote.* Edited by Carol O'Hare, Troutdale, OR: NewSage Press, 1995, 76. Edited from original edition first published in 1920.

Page 122: *Knitting Is Allowed*—"I don't ask you to stop marching entirely . . ."

"Militants Go to Jail: Refuse to Pay Fines or Stop White House Picketing." *Washington Post*, July 7, 1917.

Page 125: *Who Holds the Power?*—truncated conversation from the court

"Suffragists Take 60-Day Sentence; Won't Pay Fines." *New York Times*, July 18, 1917.

Page 157: *What to Do with Us*—"As an unenfranchised class, we have nothing to do with the making of the laws which have put us in this position." (This part of the quote is verbatim. The rest of it is added on.)

"Another Administration Retreat." *Suffragist* 5, no. 90 (1917): 5.

Page 163: *Strength*—"All the officers here know . . ."

"The Prison Notes of Rose Winslow: Smuggled to Friends from the District Jail." *Suffragist* 5, no. 97 (1917): 6.

Page 179: *Respect for the Elderly*—"I have a man here . . ."

Nolan, Mary A. "'That Night of Terror' November 14, 1917." *Suffragist* 5, no. 97 (1917): 7–8.

Page 196: *Hunger*—"They think there is nothing in our souls . . ."

Irwin, Inez Haynes. *The Story of the Woman's Party*. New York: Harcourt, Brace and Company, 1921, 276.

Page 211: *The Verdict*—"If three days ago . . ."

"Government Forced to Release Suffrage Prisoners from Occoquan." *Suffragist* 5, no. 97 (1917): 4–5.

Page 219: *When Sleep Doesn't Come*—"Thanksgiving this year . . ."

"Jail Is Calm and Peaceful Again, As 22 Suffragettes Are Released; Real Thanksgiving for Dr. Zinkham." *Washington Post*, November 28, 1917.

Page 237: *Celebrating Inez*—all quotes

Stevens, Doris. *Jailed for Freedom: American Women Win the Vote*. Edited by Carol O'Hare. Troutdale, OR: NewSage Press, 1995, 142. Edited from original edition first published in 1920.

Page 240: *The Breaking Point*—"Women cannot be law-breakers . . ."

Irwin, Inez Haynes. *The Story of the Woman's Party*. New York: Harcourt, Brace and Company, 1921, 358.

Page 241: *Wilson Relents*—"We have made partners . . ."

Wilson, Woodrow. "Address to the Senate," September 30, 1918. www.presidency.ucsb.edu/documents/address-the-senate-the -nineteenth-amendment.

Page 249: *Behind the Banners*—"We asked him for the vote . . ."

*Suffragist* (November 10, 1917). In *Treacherous Texts: An Anthology of U.S. Suffrage Literature, 1846–1946*, edited by Mary Chapman and Angela Mills, 280–281. New Brunswic, NJ: Rutgers University Press, 2012.

Page 259: *Picket Day 722*—"President Wilson is deceiving the world . . ."

"The Watchfire." *Suffragist* 7, no. 51 (1919): 6.

Page 263: *Picket Day 728*—"Being free . . ."

"Tells Milan Guarantees Are Asked By Labor." *Washington Post*, January 7, 1919.

Page 279: *Suffrage Won*—"Nothing has given me more pleasure . . ."

"Laud Women Voters." *Washington Post*, August 27, 1920.

## Places to Visit

### Belmont-Paul House, Washington, DC

*www.nps.gov/bepa/index.htm*

This museum is full of National Woman's Party artifacts. Just behind the Capitol building, it was the last headquarters of the NWP.

### Lafayette Square and the White House, Washington, DC

*www.whitehouse.gov/*

*www.gsa.gov/real-estate/historic-preservation/explore-historic
-buildings/heritage-tourism/our-capital/lafayette-square*

Lafayette Square is a public park surrounded by buildings, including the buildings that once housed Cameron House, Jackson Place, and the Belasco Theater. You can see how short a distance the suffragists were to the White House gates, where the protests on Pennsylvania Avenue were each day.

### Lucy Burns Museum at Occoquan Workhouse, Occoquan, Virginia

*www.workhousearts.org/lucyburnsmuseum/*

This newly renovated museum features the stories of the women who were tortured and imprisoned at Occoquan. It lies south of Washington, DC.

# For Further Reading

## Picture Books

Boxer, Elisa, and Vivien Mildenberger. *The Voice that Won the Vote: How One Woman's Words Made History.* Ann Arbor, MI: Sleeping Bear Press, 2020.

Gillibrand, Kirsten, and Maira Kalman. *Bold & Brave: Ten Heroes Who Won Women the Right to Vote.* New York: Alfred A. Knopf, 2018.

Robbins, Dean, and Nancy Zhang. *Miss Paul and the President: The Creative Campaign for Women's Right to Vote.* New York: Alfred A. Knopf, 2016.

Rockliff, Mara, and Hadley Hooper. *Around America to Win the Vote: Two Suffragists, a Kitten, and 10,000 Miles.* Somerville, MA: Candlewick Press, 2016.

Rosenstock, Barb, and Sarah Green. *Fight of the Century: Alice Paul Battles Woodrow Wilson for the Vote.* New York: Calkins Creek, 2020.

## Middle Grade

Bailey, Diane. *Ida B. Wells: Discovering History's Heroes.* New York: Aladdin, 2019.

Bartoletti, Susan Campbell, and Ziyue Chen. *How Women Won the Vote: Alice Paul, Lucy Burns, and their Big Idea.* New York: HarperCollins, 2020.

Howell, Senator Janet, Theresa Howell, Kylie Akia, and Alexandra Bye. *Leading the Way: Women in Power.* Somerville, MA: Candlewick Press, 2019.

Kennedy, Nancy B., and Katy Dockrill. *Women Win the Vote! 19 for the 19th Amendment.* New York: Norton Young Readers, 2020.

Messner, Kate. *History Smashers: Women's Right to Vote.* New York: Random House Books for Young Readers, 2020.

Roberts, David. *Suffragette: The Battle for Equality.* Somerville, MA: Walker Books US, 2019.

Weiss, Elaine. *The Woman's Hour (Adapted for Young Readers): Our Fight for the Right to Vote*. New York: Random House Books for Young Readers, 2020.

## Young Adult Books

Bausum, Anne. *With Courage and Cloth: Winning the Fight for a Woman's Right to Vote*. Glendale, CA: National Geographic Kids, 2004.

Conkling, Winifred. *Votes for Women! American Suffragists and the Battle for the Ballot*. New York: Algonquin Young Readers, 2018.

Dionne, Evette. *Lifting as We Climb: Black Women's Battle for the Ballot Box*. New York: Viking Books for Young Readers, 2020.

Jenkins, Tommy, and Kati Lacker. *Drawing the Vote: An Illustrated Guide to Voting in America*. New York: Abrams ComicArts, 2020.

Kops, Deborah. *Alice Paul and the Fight for Women's Rights: From the Vote to the Equal Rights Amendment*. New York: Calkins Creek, 2017.

Rubin, Susan Goldman. *Give Us the Vote! Over 200 Years of Fighting for the Ballot*. New York: Holiday House, 2020.

Smith, Erin Geiger. *Thank You for Voting Young Readers' Edition: The Past, Present, and Future of Voting*. New York: Quill Tree Books, 2020.

# Selected Bibliography

This is a condensed version of the major sources I used.

## Newspapers

I used newspapers of the time from 1913 to 1920.

*Washington Post*
*New York Times*
*Washington Herald*

## Suffragist Publications

The *Suffragist* was the official National Woman's Party publication. I utilized hundreds of articles ranging from 1913 to 1919. They are available online at the Gerritsen Collection: Women's History Online.

## Exhibits

I went to exhibits at multiple museums in Virginia and Washington, DC.

National Archives
Smithsonian National Museum of American History
Library of Congress
Virginia Museum of History and Culture
Woodrow Wilson Presidential Library and Birthplace
Workhouse Prison Museum at Lorton (now called the Lucy Burns Museum)

## Library of Congress

I utilized hundreds of photographs the Library of Congress has made available online that cover the suffrage movement.

## Papers

Papers of the National Woman's Party in the Manuscript Division, Library of Congress

Matilda Young Papers, Duke University

## Women and Social Movements Database

*https://search.alexanderstreet.com/wass*

I utilized the biographical sketches of the following women: Matilda Young, Joy Young, Rose Winslow, Alice Paul, Lucy Burns, and Hazel Hunkins.

## Yearbooks

The Washingtoniana Yearbook Collection from the People's Archive of the DC Public Library has yearbooks from Matilda Young's high school. I was able to review the "Brecky" editions from 1913 to 1916.

## Magazines

*Smithsonian Magazine*
*Notes on Virginia*
*Prologue*
*American Heritage*
*Scribner's Magazine*
*American History*

## Presentations/Talks

I attended talks about woman suffrage in person and via webcast at many institutions. They helped to give context for the full suffrage movement. I attended a few that were really focused on the time period and the women I was writing about:

Woman Suffrage Walking Tour, Washington, DC, National Women's History Museum

Occoquan Workhouse, Centennial Remembrance of the Night of Terror 1917

## "American Experience" PBS Documentaries

Ferrari, Michelle, dir. *The Vote*. Aired October 21 (Part 1) and 28 (Part 2), 2023, on PBS.

Ives, Stephen, Amanda Pollak, and Rob Rapley, dirs. *The Great War*. Aired June 19 (Part 1), June 26 (Part 2), and July 3 (Part 3), 2018, on PBS.

Pollak, Ruth, dir. *One Woman, One Vote*. Aired February 15, 1995, on PBS. Videocassette (VHS), 141 min.

## Other Papers

Bland, Sidney. "Techniques of Persuasion: The National Woman's Party and Woman Suffrage, 1913–1919." Diss., George Washington University, 1972.

Woodrow Wilson's speeches available from Woodrow Wilson Presidential Library and American Presidency Project.

## Books

Cooney, Robert P. J. *Winning the Vote: The Triumph of the American Woman Suffrage Movement*. Half Moon Bay, CA: American Graphic Press, 2005.

Irwin, Inez Haynes. *The Story of the Woman's Party*. New York: Harcourt, Brace and Company, 1921.

Roberts, Rebecca Boggs. *Suffragists in Washington, D.C.: The 1913 Parade and the Fight for the Vote*. Charleston, SC: History Press, 2017.

Southard, Belinda Stillion. *Militant Citizenship: Rhetorical Strategies of the National Woman's Party, 1913–1920*. College Station: Texas A&M University Press, 2011.

Stevens, Doris. *Jailed for Freedom: American Women Win the Vote.* Edited by Carol O'Hare. Troutdale, OR: NewSage Press, 1995. Edited from original edition first published in 1920.

Stovall, James Glen. *Seeing Suffrage: The Washington Suffrage Parade of 1913, Its Pictures, and Its Effect on the American Political Landscape.* Knoxville: University of Tennessee Press, 2013.

Terborg-Penn, Rosalyn. *African American Women in the Struggle for the Vote, 1850–1920.* Bloomington: Indiana University Press, 1998.

Terrell, Mary Church. *A Colored Woman in a White World.* Amherst, MA: Humanity Books, 2005.

# Acknowledgments

It takes a lot of people to usher a book into the world. I'm so grateful for the people who believed in *One Step Forward* enough to bring it to you, the reader.

First and foremost, this book would simply not exist without my agent, Roseanne Wells. Roseanne saw promise in this book when it wasn't even Matilda's story yet. We worked through many iterations, and if she ever doubted this would become a book, she didn't show it. Roseanne, thank you!

Monica Perez, thank you for believing in Matilda's story and bringing it to Versify. Your vision for this book made it so much better.

To Mikayla Lawrence, production editor, and Jill Amack, copy editor, for your keen eyes on my manuscript—thank you for your attention to detail!

I'm so stunned by the beautiful cover art by Babeth Lafon and designer Catherine Lee. Thank you for making Matilda come to life.

To Kenena Spalding at the Lucy Burns Museum (before it had its new location and name), thank you for taking the time to answer my questions and emails when I was at the beginning of this journey.

My critique group, Liza, Leah, and Christina—your insights, phone calls, voice memos, detailed notes, and cheerleading kept me going when I couldn't find my way through this story. Thank you for believing in me and encouraging me.

For my Nevermores gals—Patricia, Rose, and Brooke (and Emeritus Nevermores Erica and Ryan), your weekly poetry feeds me, challenges me, and makes me a better poet. It's an amazing thing when you find a group that loves words as much as you do!

My parents always made sure our house was overflowing with books—it paved the way for me to be a writer and librarian. I was so lucky to have notebooks to fill. Thanks, Mom and Dad, for your never-ending encouragement.

My husband, Donnie, first introduced me to the Occoquan

Workhouse and suggested I write a book about the women who suffered there. Little did he know that we'd be living with that story for many years. Thank you for picking up all the slack when I have writing to do. And to my kids, who have grown up with a mom who is always working on a story, thanks for sleeping in so I could write in the mornings. My vote will always be for you.